EXPLORERS INTO INFINITY

AND

THE GIANT WORLD

BY RAY CUMMINGS

COVER BY FRANK R. PAUL

Altus Press
2023

EXPLORERS INTO INFINITY

FOREWORD

Some of my present readers will doubtless remember *The Girl in the Golden Atom*. When I wrote that book of the realm of infinite smallness there was in my mind its logical converse, the realm of the infinitely large. The one a complement to the other. And so I offer *Explorers Into Infinity,* in no sense as a sequel to *The Girl in The Golden Atom,* for fictionally they have no connection, but rather as its companion story.

You will find here a complete theory of the material universe as I conceive it may perhaps really be. To my own imagination—and I think very likely to your own—it is difficult to conceive of an infinite distance beyond the stars—empty Space stretching out forever. Nor is Einstein more satisfying to me, rather less so, for out beyond the Einstein system of curved Space most lie something or nothing. It is the nothingness which puzzles me. I have tried vainly to imagine a realm, infinitely large, of unending nothingness. Time is equally puzzling. I can conceive of eventful eons lying ahead of us; but rob that time of its future events and I flounder. To me at least, the conception of Time with nothing ever happening anywhere is impossible. To me also, an event presupposes the existence of something; and so, in my effort to imagine the infinitely large—Space illimitable,

Time unending—I am forced to conceive what must fill that Space, what must happen to create that time.

You may call this tale fantastic, weird, bizarre. Doubtless it is. But with our most powerful microscopes reaching inward so tiny a distance to see no end in infinite smallness; our greatest telescopes groping futilely out into largeness unending to our vision, what is left but our imagination? And that, at least, we can send winging into the infinite!

I would not have you fear from this foreword that my story may be some pedantic, heavily technical exposition. It is not; for it is fiction only—a romance with which to entertain you; an effort, by using fictional methods, to reduce theories purely imaginative into concrete form with as great a degree of plausibility as may be. It is this only I desire: to carry you with me as you read; to make plausible this flight of our imaginations momentarily set free from the tiny everyday universe which is all we have physically to envisage.

RAY CUMMINGS

1

FREEDOM IN TIME AND SPACE

I was busy with the Martian mail which had just arrived when the message from Brett Gryce reached me. I did not apprehend that there was anything of secrecy about it, since he was using the open air; yet there was in his voice a note of tenseness and his summons was urgent.

"I can't come, Brett, until I get through the mail." I was rushed, and in a mood of ill-temper at the universe in general.

"When will that be?" he demanded

"I don't know. It's accursedly large. Most of it seems to call for radio distribution—these Martians are always in a hurry."

"Come when you can," he said quietly.

"Tonight?"

"Yes—tonight. No matter how late—I must see you, Frank."

"I'll come," I said, and cut him off.

It was long past trinight, with dawn beginning to brighten the sky beyond the masonry of lower Great-New York, when I had disposed of those miserable Martian dispatches. The Gryces lived in the Southern Pennsylvania area. My aerocar was at hand. I had rather planned to use it; but I was tired and in no mood for effort. I decided to take the pneumatic, since there was a branch—little traveled, it is true—which would drop me within some twenty kilometers of the Gryce home.

They gave me an individual cylinder, with a bed if I cared to sleep. I did not. I lay there wondering what Brett could want of me; pleased also that I would see Francine—dear little Frannie....

EXPLORERS INTO INFINITY
by Ray Cummings.

The vehicle was out of control, pushing at the house like a great white giant.

Occasionally I would call the Director ahead. They are sometimes careless in the switching of special individual cylinders; and I had no wish to pass the branch and find myself bringing up at some gulf terminal with half the morning getting back. Once I called Brett. He would meet me with his aero at the end of the branch when I arrived. He, too, reminded the Director. A surly sort of fellow; the Gryces had already reported him to the General Traffic Staff of Great-London.

I was not misdirected, however; but it was broad daylight when I emerged to find Brett impatiently awaiting me. And in a few minutes more we were landing at the aero-stage beside the Gryce home.

It was a simple enough place—for all Dr. Gryce's reputed wealth. An estate of a few kilometers, set in a heavy grove of trees with a high metallic wall about it. The granite house itself was small, unpretentious. There were few outbuildings;

one a large rectangular affair which vaguely I understood was a workshop. I had never been in it. I knew old Dr. Gryce was interested in science; in his day he had materially advanced civilization with several fundamental devices. But what—if anything—he might be doing now, I had no idea.

Brett would tell me nothing beyond the fact that his father had suggested they send for me. But he seemed excited, tense. Dr. Gryce greeted me with his familiar kindliness. Though I did not see as much of this family as I would like (my business with the Interplanetary Mails was wholly underpaid and miserably confining), yet I counted the Gryces among my closest friends.

Dr. Gryce said, "We are very glad to see you, Frank. Come outside. Frannie is preparing breakfast."

His manner was grave and quiet as always. But there was about him also an air of tenseness; and an aspect of apprehension. And it struck me, a sort of weary, resigned depression which suddenly made his years sit more heavily upon him. He was a man of some eighty odd; and though for him no more than twenty or thirty years of life could be anticipated, I had never considered him really old. He was small, slight of frame, but erect, sturdy and vigorous. A smooth-shaven face with no more lines upon it than a keen intellect and a character once wholly forceful would engrave. And a mass of snow-white shaggy hair to make his head appear preternaturally large.

He seemed old now, however, with that sense of depression hanging upon him. And an indefinable aspect of fear.

I must allot a word to picture the three children of Dr. Gryce, motherless since childhood. Brett was now twenty-eight—three years older than myself, and physically my opposite. I am short, slender and rather dark. And—so they tell me—not too even of temper. Brett was a blond young giant. Crisp, wavy blond hair, blue eyes and the strong-featured, ruddy face of a handsome athlete. But not too handsome, for there was upon him no consciousness of his essentially masculine beauty. He was wonderfully good-natured. His was a ready, hearty laugh. He looked at life often from the humorous viewpoint. But he had also a touch of his father's grave dignity; and a keen intellect and a soberness of thought and reason far beyond his years.

The two other children—Martynn and Francine—were twins, now just seventeen. Alike, physically and temperamentally, as children of such a birth traditionally should be. Slim and rather small—Martynn about my height; Francine somewhat shorter. Both blue-eyed, with blond hair. Francine's hair was long-waving tresses which she wore generally in plaits over her shoulders; Martynn's was short and curly; They were rather alike of feature; a delicacy of mold which gave to Martynn a girlishness. But not an effeminacy, for he was a young daredevil; and his sister hardly a lesser one. In childhood and adolescence an impish spirit of deviltry had always seemed to possess these twins; a spirit of mischief which had made them a great trial to their father. It had turned, now that they were nearing maturity, into an apparent desire for reckless adventure—the product of abounding health, and bubbling, irrepressible good nature. They adored each other; were constantly together, with youthful escapades threatening limb and life and complete disaster, out of which they would emerge—or be extricated—with dauntless spirits unperturbed.

The greater maturity of womanhood at seventeen had brought to Frannie moments of gentleness, sweetness and a simple dignity. But they were brief moments, and no more than a word or look from her twin was needed to dispel them. Martt himself was without a vestige of dignity. But they were no fools, these twins. They could, upon strict necessity, give sober, intelligent thought to any problem at hand (Martynn had won honors at the Great-London University); but of sober, matured action they were incapable. Fearless—unreasonably fearless. But irresistible, likable, and apparently quite capable of being restrained. A word from Dr. Gryce, or from Brett—and to a lesser extent from me who had known them from childhood—brought instant though often very temporary obedience. They considered themselves quite grown up now. In truth, at seventeen, Frannie was to my eyes a really beautiful young woman.

We sat in a little arbor beside the house, with its breakfast table already laid. Dr. Gryce, Brett, and myself. Martt was with Frannie preparing the meal. It was evidence of the simplicity which marked the Gryce household. In these days of mechanical devices for almost everything—and the usual multiplicity of servants—there was not a meal prepared for Dr. Gryce save by his daughter.

I was very curious to learn why they had sent for me; but I had no need to question, for at once Dr. Gryce plunged into it.

"I hope, Frank, that you can stay—well, at least a few days with us. Can you?"

I stared. The Day Officer of the Manhattan Interplanetary Postal Division was undoubtedly already in a rage at my absence. I said so. "A few days? Dr. Gryce, I dread every conjunction that brings these accursed mails—my divisional officers think it's a crime even to eat or sleep when a planet is near us."

He smiled. "I imagine I can fix it."

"Then I'll stay, of course. If you could fix the planetary orbits so that they were parabolas, Dr. Gryce, it would suit me exactly."

He and Brett both were smiling but Dr. Greece's smile was

momentary, for at once that indefinable air of trouble returned to him.

"Frank," he said, "I hardly know how to begin telling you what we have done—are about to do. It seems curious also—I know it will strike you so, you have been such friend to me and my children—that during all these years we have given you no hint of our purpose."

"We have told no one," Brett put in: "no one in the world."

I said nothing, but my curiosity increased. It was doubtless of grave import, this thing they had to tell me; the solemnity, earnestness which stamped them both was unmistakable

For a moment Dr. Gryce was silent; then he said abruptly, "You know, Frank, all my life I have been engaged with science. In a measure I have been successful; there are a few devices which will bear my name when I am gone."

I nodded. "I know that very well Dr. Gryce."

"But all those things," he added earnestly, "all that I stand for to the world, has really been of little importance to me. My main labor, goal, dream, if you will, I have never told anyone—not a living person except my children. For ten years past Brett has been helping me. And though you would hardly believe it for the last year or two Martt and Frannie have been of material aid in the accomplishment of my purpose."

"What branch of science?" I asked. "And you've accomplished it? You're ready to give it to the world?"

"Accomplished it—yes. But we are not ready to give it to the world—perhaps we never shall. There would be evil in it—evil diabolical—in untrained or unscrupulous hands. But we are ready to test it—a practical test. Tonight, Frank, my boy Brett is going upon an adventure—"

The fear which had been lurking in his eyes leaped to stamp his other features. He was afraid for Brett—afraid of this thing they were going to do. He had stopped abruptly; and more quietly he added:

"I want you to understand me, Frank, and so for a moment we must be wholly theoretical. This thing we are about to do involves the construction of our whole material universe. You know, of course, that no limit has been found to the divisibility of matter?"

His sudden question confused me. "You mean," I stammered, "that things can be infinitely small?"

"That there is no limit to smallness," Brett put in. "An atom—an electron—they are mere words. Within them conceivably might be a space with stars, planets, suns—worlds of their own so tiny that compared to the Space in which they roam that Space would seem—and would be—illimitable. Picture that, Frank. And picture upon one of those world's inhabitants of proportionate smallness. What would they see, feel or think of the universe? Would they not conceive it about as we do? Picture them with powerful microscopes, looking downward into the matter composing their world. They would be aware of molecules, atoms—they would gaze down into Space unending. Another realm within their own. And within that one—others and yet others to infinity. The conception confuses you, Frank? It need not. Each of those realms is tiny—or large—according to the viewpoint. There can be no such thing as absolute size."

"That is what I mean," Dr. Gryce interrupted eagerly. "Absolute size—how can you conceive it? You cannot.

A thing is large or small only in relation to something else smaller or larger."

He waved his hand to the rolling landscape with the morning light and shadow upon it, visible through the arbor.

"There is our everyday world, Frank. How big is it? You can

not say. Millimeters, meters, kilometers, helans, light-years—
those are only words with which we designate a comparison.
Compared to what our microscopes show us, this world of ours
is very large, but compared to the spaces between the stars—
the stars themselves—it is very small. Try then to imagine its
absolute size. You can not, because there is no such thing. A
universe within what we call an atom—another realm within
an atom of matter upon one of the worlds of *that* universe—
is not an extraordinary state of smallness *until we compare it
with ourselves.*

"And this world of ours. It is normal to us; of no absolute
size whatever—neither large nor small—until we compare
it to something else. But suppose we visualize larger realms?
Suppose we say these planets, stars—all the starry universe
within our ken and this visual space which contains them—
suppose we imagine all that to be contained within the atom
of a particle of matter of some comparatively still larger realm?
At once our world and ourselves shrink into smallness. Where
a moment ago we had seemed large, now we seem small. Yet
that other gigantic world within which we are contained—if
we could live in it our telescopes would show us still larger
Space unending. We would feel tiny—and of actuality *we
would be tiny*—contemplating Space and size so much larger."

"And there you have infinity of Space," Brett added, as his
father paused. "Unending Space both smaller and larger than
ourselves. We—everything of which we can be physically
aware—represent no more than a single step in the ladder
which has no bottom nor no top. You can not conceive an end
in either direction. There is no such thing. Nor—as Father
says—can you declare anything to be small or large considered by itself alone. This then is Space as we conceive it to be.
Illimitable, unending—infinite Space."

The conception momentarily seemed wholly beyond my grasp. What I would have answered when for a moment Dr. Gryce and Brett paused I do not know, for from the house the approaching voices of Martt and Frannie reached us.

"You'll fall, I tell you! Frannie, give me that!"

"I won't."

"You'll trip over the wires and you'll fall and smash it!"

"I won't."

The sound of a crash. And Martt's voice, "There, I told you!"

They were upon us, wheeling the tray laden with breakfast; Martt, flushed, laughing. "Oh, hello, Frank—they didn't switch you wrong, did they? Frannie broke the heater coils—if the breakfast gets cold, don't blame me."

And Frannie, also flushed and laughing and a trifle rueful over the mishap. Dressed in a blue blouse and widely flaring, knee-length trousers, with her golden hair tossing on her shoulders. The picture of a little housewife, of early morning informality. I thought I had never seen her so beautiful.

"That, Frank, is our conception of the infinity of Space."

With breakfast finished Brett had resumed the discussion. We were all seated in the arbor. Martt and Frannie momentarily were quiet, seemingly keenly interested in the impression upon me which they anticipated would come from their father's disclosures.

Dr. Gryce said, "The idea of Time unending is indissolubly bound with the concept of infinite Space, you will realize, Frank, for some centuries it has been understood that Time and Space are inextricably blended. We think instinctively of Space as a tangible entity—of length, breadth and thickness. And of Time as intangible. Such really is not the case. Space has three dimensions—but Time also has a dimension."

"Length," Martt put in."It sounds like a play on words, but—"

"It isn't," Frannie finished for him. "I can't imagine anything clearer than that Time has length

Dr. Gryce ignored them. "You must understand also that Time as we conceive it can not exist except as the measurement of a *length* between two events. And what is an event? It presupposes the existence of *Matter,* does it not? Matter thus is introduced into the universe. It also can not be independent of Time and Space. So long as anything material exists, there must be Space for it to exist in; and Time to mark the passing of its existence.

"Of our universe, then, we now have Matter, Time and Space. There is a fourth—shall I say, element?" It also is interdependent with each of the other three. It is *Motion.* You know, of course, that there can be no such thing as absolute Motion."

"Or absolute Time," Frannie put in.

"That we will discuss later," Dr. Gryce said quickly, "since it is more intricate of conception. Absolute Motion is impossible and non-existence. We can say a thing moves fast or slowly, *only in relation to the movement of something else.* One word more. I want you to realize, Frank, how wholly dependent each of these factors is upon the other. *Matter,* for instance, is an entity persisting in Space and Time, *Motion* is the simultaneous change of the position of Matter in Space and Time. A thing was *here, then;* it is *there, now.* That is Motion. You see how you can not deal with one without involving the others?"

"Say, Father, why don't you tell him what we're going to do?" Martt demanded. "Frank, listen—tonight Brett and I—"

"But I'm going, too," Frannie declared.

"You're not!"

I saw again that look of fear in old Dr. Gryce's eyes. His children—the spirit of youth with its lust for adventure—they were eager and excited. But Dr. Gryce saw beyond that—saw the danger....

He said gravely, "There is no possibility of my making you understand the details, Frank, until we have gone into the matter thoroughly. But as Martt implies, you are no doubt impatient. I will tell you then, briefly, that for most of my life I have been delving into this subject—Matter, Space, Time and Motion illimitable. Longing to investigate this immense material universe which I believe exists. But we humans are fettered, Frank. Like an ant, living for a brief moment enchained with a cobweb to a twig and trying to envisage the earth."

His voice now was trembling with emotion. "I was satisfied to see with my own eyes some little part into infinity. I invented what we—my children and I—call the myrdoscope. I will explain it presently. Suffice it now to say that there are normally invisible rays, akin to light, crossing Space, and I have made them visible. We captured them—saw after a myriad trials unavailing, occasional vague glimpses of the beyond which came to us. It might have satisfied me, but three years ago one night, Brett saw—"

He paused, looking at Brett. Martt and Frannie were breathless, with eyes fixed on me.

Brett said, and his voice had a queer, solemn hush to it, "I was looking through the myrdoscope. "We had seen blurred, brief glimpses of a realm—"

"Beyond the stars," Frannie breathed.

"Yes, beyond the stars. A realm seemingly of forest, or something growing. Silvery patches—you might imagine they were water, or light shining upon something that glistened. They were always haphazard, these glimpses. We caught them, not always from one direction—seemingly from everywhere. A realm encompassing—enclosing—our whole star-filled Space.

"With the labor of years, which you, Frank, will appreciate to some degree, Father has charted what for our own little ken we might call absolute points in Space. Landmarks, say, of this outer realm. With our whirling earth, the ever-changing planets and stars, only this outer realm seemed of fixed position. We could sometimes return our gaze to the same landmark—a tremendous crescent-shaped patch of silver, for instance, which several times we succeeded in re-finding.

"It was near this patch at which I was one night gazing, when through some vagary of the ray bearing its image—or some difference in our crude apparatus—the scene suddenly clarified. And magnified as though at once I had leaped a million light-years toward it.

"I saw then a magnified section of the larger scene. The patch of silver appeared now as a shimmering, opalescent liquid. A segment of shore-front; and this all in a moment, again magnified. Upon a bluish bank of soft vegetation, with the opal liquid beside it, I saw a girl half reclining. A girl of human form, but transfigured by a beauty more than human, A girl of a civilization behind our own—or perhaps one in advance—I do not know. She was robed in a short, simple garment more like a glistening, glowing silver veil than a dress. Her hair was long—a tangled dark mass. She reclined there in an attitude of ease and the abandonment of maidenly solitude. I say that she was more than beautiful—oh, Frank—"

Brett's voice had suddenly lost the precise exactitude of the scientist. He seemed to have forgotten his father—Martt and Frannie; it was as though he were confiding his human emotions only to me.

"Beautiful, Frank. A strange, wild beauty, with a curious ethereal aspect to it. I don't know—it's indescribable. Human—half human, but half divine."

He checked himself; the scientist in him again became uppermost; but though he now spoke with careful phrasing, his face remained flushed.

"It was some moments before I saw additional details. And then I realized that the girl was not alone. Upon her bare feet were a sort of sandal with thongs crossing the ankle. And standing there beside one of her feet were two tiny human figures. In height, the length perhaps of her little foot. Men of human form; yet queerly grotesque; misshapen. One of them was in the act of reaching upward toward the tassel of her sandal cord where it dangled from her ankle; reaching as though to grasp it and draw himself upward. The other was watching; and both were grinning with gnomelike malevolence.

"Nor was this all, for behind the girl, a brief distance away in what appeared a woodland dell, was another figure—a man of aspect akin to the grinning gnomes, save that in comparative size even to the girl he was gigantic. Ten times her height perhaps, he stood behind her towering into the trees about him, A man of short, squat legs, dark with matted hair; a garment like the gnomes, which might have been an animal skin; a heavy massive chest; black hair long to his neck. A face with clipped hair upon it. He was regarding the girl; a grin, but with a leer to it—horribly sinister. And in his great hands, brandished like a bludgeon, was an uprooted tree.

"Have I given you an idea of motion in the scene? There was none. The girl was obviously wholly unaware that she was not alone. She lay motionless. But the lack of movement in her— in them all—was more marked than that. The girl's lips were parted in a half-smile of revery; but the outlines of her bosom beneath the silver veil did not move. There was no movement of breath, no change of expression. The gnomes, the giant— not the minutest change could I see mirrored in their faces.

"Yet it was so lifelike, I could not doubt it was life—and that the motion was there though I could not see it. I watched all night, shaken with this fragment of drama, perhaps tragedy, which I was witnessing—but even the girl's eyelids did not tremble. Dawn came; the scene faded.

"For a month I did not even tell Father; and Frank, the vision of that girl has never left me. The menace—gruesome, sinister—upon her—and her beauty—"

"Haven't you ever seen her again?" I asked eagerly. "Was it life? How could it be life without motion?"

"Oh, he saw her again," Martt exclaimed. "I've seen her—we've all seen her."

"Tell him, Brett," Frannie urged.

"A month before I even told Father. During it, I searched for the scene unavailing, then Father and I searched together. It was a year, when almost from the same orbital position we came upon the scene again. A year—and now we saw a change. The figures all were there, frozen into immobility as before. But the gnome had caught the tassel, had drawn himself partly up to stand upon the girl's white ankle. The giant had come a trifle forward, and the upraised tree in his hands was partly lowered. The girl's attitude was unchanged, but there was now upon her face the vague dawn of startled knowledge, as though at that instant she was becoming aware of something pulling at her sandal cord, something touching her ankle—perhaps too, she was hearing a sound from the giant behind her. The startled knowledge which as yet had not had time fully to register upon her face."

My mind was whirling with a confusion of thoughts; the vague comprehension of what Brett meant was coming to me. I stammered, "Not yet had time—but Brett, you must have watched them all that night—"

"That night, Frank. And others—but there was no sign of movement. Another year—that was last year—we saw the girl partly aware of her danger. This year—a month ago—she was fully aware of it, Frightened—her eyes stricken wide with terror. But she had had no time as yet to move.

"Don't you understand, Frank? That drama is going on out there now. Like size of Matter and Space—and rate of Motion—there is no absolute Time. It is all comparative. To that realm out there of which we have been given a little vision, our tiny worlds here in the heavens are mere whirling electrons, like the electrons within one of our own atoms which to our consciousness of Time revolve many times a second.

"A year! A single revolution of our earth about its sun! To that girl out there, what we call a year is merely an electron in a fraction of a second revolving about its fellow. Even that is very slow—for she herself is wholly within the atom of a greater world outside her. A year as we call it—a second or less, to her. And though she is in full movement, how can we hope to see it by watching for a night? If a year were a second to her—an eight-hour vigil of ours would encompass less than a thousandth part of a second of her life!

"All comparative, Frank. There is nothing wonderful or really strange about it. In what we would experience to be a hundred years from now that girl will be fully faced with the menace of her assailants. A moment only, to her consciousness. It is that, Frank, we meant by the infinity of Time."

"Tell him what we're going to do," Martt insisted breathlessly.

It came from Brett in a burst almost incoherent. "I was not satisfied merely to see into this comparative infinity. Nor was Father. We have worked three feverish years, Frank, to climax all the labor of Father's which had gone before. And we have found a way—not merely to see, but to transport ourselves into these greater realms. A vehicle—I'll show you—explain it all. Its size can be changed—the state of the matter composing it is within our control. Its position in Space can be changed—simple enough, Frank, to enlarge upon the principles of our interplanetary vehicles. And—with one factor so interdependent upon the other—we have been able to control the rate of its Time-progress. It travels through Time as it does through Space."

His words were tumbling over each other. "You'll see it in a moment, Frank—test it—we have it here, ready yesterday. It sets us free, don't you understand? Free at last in Space and Time. And I'm going in it tonight—with Martt perhaps—we're going out to reach that girl upon an equality of Size and Time-progress. Going out to explore infinity!"

2

"THIS COULD DESTROY THE UNIVERSE"

I had anticipated that they would show me a vehicle similar perhaps to the huge and elaborate space-flyers in the service of our Interplanetary Postal Division. But instead of taking me to the workshops where I had conceived it to be lying—serene, glistening with newness, intricate with what devices for its changing of size and Time-rate I could not imagine—instead of this they took me into the house. And there, in Dr. Gryce's quiet study with its sober, luxurious furnishings and his library of cylinders ranged in orderly array about the walls, I saw not one but four machines—mere models standing there on the polished table-top. Four of them identical—all of a milk-white metal.

But they were models complete in every detail. I stood beside one, regarding it with a breathless, absorbed interest as Dr. Gryce commented upon it. A cube of about the length of my forearm in its three equal dimensions with a cone-shaped tower on top—a little tower not much longer than my longest finger. The cube itself had a rectangular doorway and in each face two banks of windows. The door slid sidewise, the windows were of a transparent material, like glass. Midway about the cube ran a tiny balcony at the second-story level. It was wholly enclosed by the glasslike material. It extended around all four sides; small doors from it gave access to the cube's interior. The cone on top also had windows, and its entire apex was transparent.

I bent down and peered into that lower doorway. Tiny rooms were there. Bedrooms; a cookery—a home complete, save that it was wholly unfurnished. The largest room on the lower story—its floor had a circular transparent pane in it—was fitted with a seemingly intricate array of tiny mechanisms all of the same milk-white metal. A metallic table held most of them; and I could see wires fine as cobwebs connecting them. And in a corner of this room, a metallic spiral stairway leading to the upper story.

Dr. Gryce said, "That is the instrument room, complete. It contains every mechanism for the operation of the vehicle. We made it in this size—large enough to facilitate construction, but it is small enough to be economical of material. This substance—we have never named it—is of our own isolation. It is expensive. I'll explain it presently.... That room beside the instrument room is where we will put the usual everyday instruments necessary to the journey. Oxygen tanks—the apparatus for air purification and air renewal; telescopes, microscopes—my myrdoscope—all that sort of thing we can best obtain in its normal size. Those—and the furnishings—the provisions—all those in their normal size we will put into it later."

You mean," I asked, "this is not a model? This is the actual vehicle?"

"Yes," he smiled.

"But there are four of them."

"We made six, Frank. It was advisable and not unduly difficult to duplicate the parts in the making. The assembling took time—"

Brett said, "Father was insistent that we make every advance test possible. We have already used two of them. We are going to test the others today."

"Now," exclaimed Frannie. "Do it now—Frank will want to see it."

Dr. Gryce lifted one of the vehicles. In his hand it seemed light as alemite. He placed it on a taboret and we sat grouped around it.

"I shall send it into Time," he said quietly, "with its size unchanged, with no motion in Space, so that always in relation to us it will remain right here—I am going to send it back into other ages of Time" He turned to me earnestly. "We wanted you here, Frank, because you are so good a friend to me and my children. But for a selfish reason as well. When Brett goes out into Space and Time tonight, I want your keen eye to follow him. Your ability to record so accurately on the clocks what you see at any given instant—"

He was referring to my experience at the Table Mountain observatory—my first work when my training period was over. I had, indeed, a curiously keen vision for astronomical observation, and a quickness of finger upon the clock to record what I saw. In transit work I was extremely accurate; even now they were asking the Postal Division for my services at Table Mountain in the forthcoming transit of Venus.

Dr. Gryce was saying, "Your accuracy is phenomenal, Frank—your figures as you observe what little we see of this flight will help me—set my mind at rest that Brett is making no errors." He ended with a smile, "So you realize we have a selfish motive in wanting you."

"I'm very glad," I responded. He nodded and went back at once to what he had been saying previously. "I'm going to send this into Time. You must understand, Frank, that I can give you now only the fundamental concepts underlying this apparatus. We have so much to do today—so little time for theory. I need only tell you that it is readily demonstrable that

Time is one of the inherent factors governing the *state of Matter*. This substance we have discovered—created, if you will— yields readily to a change of state. An electronic charge—a current akin to, but not identical with electricity—changes the state of this substance in several ways. A rapid duplication of the fundamental entities within its electrons—they are, as you perhaps know, mere *whirlpools of nothingness*—this rapid duplication adds size. The substance—with shape unaltered—grows larger. With such a size-change there comes a normal, correspondingly progressive change of Time-rate. We had to go beyond that, however, and secure an independent Time-rate, independently changeable, so that the vehicle might remain quiescent in size and still change its Time. In doing that, the state of the matter as our senses perceive it is completely altered. As you know, no two bodies can occupy the same space at the same time. Which only means that with the Time-dimensions identical, different dimensions of Space are needed. With the Time-dimension differing—the state of Matter is different; two bodies thus can be together in the same space."

"What is a Time-dimension?" I asked. "I mean—how can you alter it?"

"I would say, Frank, that the Time-dimension of a material body is the *length*—or a measure of the length—of its fundamental vibration. Basically there is no real substance as we conceive it—for all Matter is mere vibration. Let us delve into substance. We find Matter consists of molecules vibrating in Space. Molecules are composed of atoms vibrating in Space. Within the atoms are electrons, revolving in Space. The electrons are without substance, merely vibrations electrically negative in character. The nucleus—once termed proton—is all then that we have left of substance. What is it? A mere vortex—an electrical vortex of nothingness!

"You see, Frank, there is no real substance existing. It is all vibration. Motion, in other words. Of what? That we do not know. Call it a motion of disembodied electrical energy. Perhaps it is something akin to that. But from it, our substantial, tangible, material universe is built. All dependent upon its vibratory rate. And the measure of that I would call the Time-dimension. When we alter that—when through the impulse of a current of vibration we attack that fundamental vortex to make it whirl at greater or lesser rate—then we, in effect, have changed the Time-dimension."

There was so much that seemed dimly close to my understanding, and yet eluded me!

"But," I said, "if you send that little cube back into Time, it will no longer exist at all. It will be in the past—non-existent now. Or suppose you send it into the future? It *will exist* sometime—but now, it will be non-existent."

"Ah, that's where you're wrong," Brett exclaimed. "Don't you realize that you're making Time absolute? You're taking yourself and this present instant as fixed points of Space and Time— the standards beyond which nothing else can exist. That's fatuous. Frank, look here, it's simple enough once you grasp it. Time and Space are quite similar, except that you have never moved about in Time but you have in Space. Suppose you had not. Suppose—with your present power of thought—you were this house. You had always been here—always would be here. Suppose, then, that the world—the land and water—moved slowly past you, at an unalterable rate. That's what Time does to us. Then, suppose I were to say to you—you as the house— 'Let us go now to Great-London.' That would puzzle you. You would say, 'Great-London was here a year ago. But now it is gone—non-existent. It did exist—but now it doesn't.' Or you would say, 'The shore of the Great Pacific Ocean will be here next year.' If I said, 'I'm going there now,' you would reply, 'But you'll be in the future. You'll be non-existent.' Making yourself the standard of everything. Don't you see how fatuous that is?"

I did not answer. It was so strange, a mode of thought; it made me feel so insignificant, so enslaved by the fetters of my human senses. And these fetters Brett was very soon to cast off.

Martt said, "Can't we make the tests, Father? There is a frightful lot to do and it's nearly mid-morning already."

From the table Dr. Gryce took a small rod of the milk-white metal—a rod half a meter long and the diameter of my smallest finger. He knelt on the floor beside the taboret, peering into the tiny doorway of the mechanism he was about to send winging into the distant ages of our Past. Again we were breathless.

"More light, Frannie," he said. "I can not see inside here." Frannie illumined the tubes along the ceiling; the room was flooded with their soft, blue-white light.

"That's better." Rod in hand he turned momentarily to me. "I'm going to throw the Time-switch by pressing it with this rod," he explained. "Within the vehicle—the continued space there—the current is equally felt." He smiled gravely. "Without the rod I should lose a finger to the Past—"

Carefully he inserted the rod into the doorway. A moment of fumbling, then I heard a click. The little milk-white model seemed to tremble. It glowed; from it there came a soft, infinitely small humming sound. It glowed, melted into translucency—transparency. For an instant I had a vague sense that a spectral wraith of it was still before me. Then with a blink of my eyelids I realized that it was gone. The taboret was empty. Beside it, Dr. Gryce knelt with the rod melted off midway of its length in his hand.

I breathed again. Brett said softly. "It is gone, Frank. Gone into the Past, relative to our consciousness of Time. Gone from our senses—yet it is here—occupying the same Space it did before—but with a different Time."

He passed his hand through the apparent vacancy above the taboret. To me then came a realization of how crowded all Space must be! Of what a tiny fraction of things existent—of events occurring—are we conscious! That Space over the taboret—empty to me... yet it held for a mind omniscient an infinity of things strewn through the ages of the Past and Future. What multiplicity of events—unseen by me—Time was loading separate in that crowded Space above the taboret!

Dr. Gryce was saying, "Let us test one now by sending it into smallness—come here, Frank."

He had risen to stand by the table, with another of the models before him. "This bit of stone," he said. "Let us send it into that."

He laid a flat piece of black-gray, smoothly polished stone on the table near the model. And with another rod he reached into the doorway. Again I heard a click. He withdrew the rod. "You see, Frank."

I saw that the rod was slightly compressed along the length he had inserted. The model was already dwindling. Soundlessly, untremblingly—it was contracting, becoming smaller, with shape and aspect otherwise unchanged. Soon it was the size of my fist. Dr. Gryce picked it up, rested it upon, his opened hand. But in a moment it was no more than a tiny cube rocking in the movement of his palm. He gripped it gingerly with thumb and forefinger and set it on the polished black slab of stone. Its milk-white color there showed it clearly. But it was very small—smaller than the nail of my little finger. The cone-shaped tower was a needle-point.

A breathless moment passed. It was now no more than a white speck upon the black stone surface.

Brett said, "Try the microscope, Frank, You watch it."

I put the low-powered instrument over it; Brett adjusted the light. The stone was smoothly polished. But now, under the glass, upon a shaggy mass of uneven rock surface I saw the vehicle visually as large as it had been originally. But it was dwindling progressively faster. Soon it lay tilted sidewise upon a slope of the rock; smaller—a tiny speck clinging there.

"Can you still see it?" Brett murmured.

"Yes—no—now it is gone." The rock seemed empty. Somewhere down in there the little mechanism lay dwindling. Forever it would grow smaller. Dwindling into an infinity of smallness; but always to be with things of its size—and things yet smaller....

As I turned from the glass, I became aware that Martt and Frannie were not in the room. Dr. Gryce and Brett, absorbed in the test, quite evidently had not noticed them leave. There had been two other models on the table—there was now but one.

Then from the garden outside the house a cry reached us. A shout—a cry of fear—terror. Martt's voice.

"Father! Brett! Help us! Help! Quick!"

We rushed from the room. Crowning wonder, yet horrible! A surge of fear swept me. In the garden quite near the house stood the other model. Small no longer. It had grown—*was growing*—until already it was as large as the house itself. Around it the flowers, shrubs, even a tree had been pushed and trampled by its expanding bulk. It stood gleaming white in the sunlight, motionless save for that steady, increasingly rapid growth. Its windows and doors loomed large dark rectangles; its balcony was broad as a corridor; its cone tower was already reared higher than the nearest trees.

"Father! Help!"

At the doorway of the vehicle, standing just outside it, were the terror—stricken Martt and Frannie. They were holding the end of a long metallic pole which projected into the doorway. Struggling with its weight, striving to throw the switch inside.

We reached them. The expanding bulk of the gleaming side of the vehicle had pushed them back into a thicket of shrubbery. Near them a tree, uprooted as though it were a straw sticking upright in sand, was pushed aside and fell with a crash.

Martt and Frannie were livid with terror; breathless, almost exhausted with their futile efforts.

Martt panted, "We can't—lift the pole! It's—too heavy—too large inside."

Within the huge doorway, by the sunlight streaming through the windows, I could see the interior half of the pole, bloated by growth, huge, heavy.

Brett shoved Frannie away. "Frank! Here—take hold with us"

Dr. Gryce was with us. Together we four men got the interior end of the pole upon the table inside. A tremendous switch lever was there But the pole slipped, rolled down... I expected it to break at the doorway point where it was so small outside, but it did not. The expanding door-way had pushed us farther back. Another tree on the other side fell. Above us the vehicle's tower loomed like a cathedral spire. Tremendous now, the vehicle had grown until it was almost touching the house. A fence had been trampled, had vanished beneath its giant bulk.

And the growth was increasing rapidly. If we could not check it.... If it got wholly beyond control—this monster, growing... forever growing, to a size infinitely large—larger than our earth itself....

I must have been standing stupidly confused. I heard Dr.

Gryce imploring, "Take hold of it, Frank. We must lift it. We must—our last chance—"

But Brett pushed us away. "I'm going inside. I can move the switch—let go of me, Father! That switch—it isn't too big yet—but it will be in a minute. Let go of me!"

"No! No, Brett! The shock as you went in—you couldn't take it so suddenly. It might hurt you—kill you. And the switch is too big for your strength."

It was out of control—this monster, growing, inexorably growing—it was pushing at the house—a great white giant pushing gently but with an irresistible power at the little toy house beside it. I could see the house shifting on its foundations; a corner of it tilted downward.

"Brett! Father! Try it now. One last try." Martt and Frannie had the pole again in position. With a last despairing effort we raised it; slid it up over the giant table-edge; caught the wide flaring side of the giant switch. Pushing—despairingly; five of us, pigmies struggling there at that giant threshold. The switch moved. Our pole held its place; the switch moved farther, clicked with a tremendous snap that reverberated about us. The growth of the monster was checked. It stood there serene, triumphant, with the little house, tilted, but still standing bravely beside it.

White, shaken, we ceased our efforts. Frannie gasped, "We—We only wanted to make it a normal size—so you could load it up with the furniture and things. But it—it got away from us."

Dr. Gryce said. "It is a lesson—perhaps a lesson which we needed forced upon us." He gestured to the great quiescent white building which had spread itself over most of the devastated garden. "A lesson," he repeated. "We must guard this power carefully. In unskilled or unscrupulous hands it is a power for evil almost unthinkable. This monster here—if it had gotten beyond us—if we had lost its control—this could destroy the Universe!"

3

EXPLORERS INTO INFINITY

"You think we've got everything in it?" Frannie asked anxiously.

We had gotten the vehicle back to a size normal to our own stature; and all day had been working to equip it. The instrument room—its Space and Time and size mechanisms were complete. I had learned now that it was to be transported through Space by very similar principles to those commonly in use—a controlled attraction or repulsion of the faces of its cube for the heavenly body nearest to it; in effect, an intensification—a neutralization—or reversal at will of the electronic force which flows between and mutually attracts all material bodies; the force which once—in centuries past—was called gravitation. It needed no word of explanation. Its velocity and distance dials, its direction indicators, were familiar, though rather more intricate than those I had seen in the Interplanetary Service. Beyond that, there was a bank of dials upon which a changing size was recorded—with the vehicle's present starting dimensions to be the standard unit. And other dials for its Time-change. Of these there were two distinct sets. One, a record of the normal Time-change, inevitable to a change of size: another, a comparison of that Time-distance with the normal Time-progress of the earth, so that the Time-position of the vehicle into the Earth's Past or Future could be seen.

In a subsidiary instrument-room was a variety of modern astronomical apparatus; the myrdoscope, and a receiver for an aural ray which, as a guide to Brett, Dr. Gryce was to send from earth. Of this, in more detail they later explained.

In a smaller room were the apparatus for air renewal, the making of various necessary gases, water and synthetic foods; a store-room of provisions; rooms furnished comfortably so that the vehicle was complete in its living quarters, A thousand details, until at the last I felt as Frannie did—wondering how we could have overlooked a score of things we had intended to do.

It was nightfall when we finished; and all that evening we spent checking up the equipment. Dr. Gryce's home had not been seriously damaged by the morning's mishap; and as midnight approached we gathered in the little observation and instrument room he had built in its upper story. Brett and Martt, it had been decided, were to make the journey; we others were to watch and wait. It seemed the more difficult role. All that evening Dr. Gryce had been increasingly silent, careworn of manner and aspect. And though Brett was excited in his mature, repressed fashion—and Martt frankly exuberant—I saw that little Frannie was solemn, perturbed as her father.

It was a soft, brilliant, cloudless night, with no moon to pale the gleaming stars. And at last every detail was settled, and the midnight hour we had set for departure was at hand. We went forth with them to the waiting vehicle. There was nothing more to say. They stood—Brett and Martt—in the opened doorway as we gathered about them.

"Well—good-bye, Father—good-bye, Frannie dear." Brett held her close; then released her, pushed her away. "Good-bye, Frank." His hand-clasp was warm and steady.

Martt was jocular, but now at the last I could hear a tremble to his voice. "When we get to that girl out there—well, I'm going to tell her how interested you all are in her." His laugh was high-pitched. "That is if we can handle that giant."

"Good-bye, Brett. Good-bye, Martt."

Our words were so futile, so inadequate to the surge of feeling within us! The door slid closed upon them. The vehicle, not to change size until it was far into the realms of outer interstellar Space, beyond our crowding little planets—lifted gently, soared upward, slid away from us, a glistening white shape up there in the quiet starlight.

Gravely, silently, with what sinking of heart I could only imagine, Dr. Gryce stood regarding it. Beside me Frannie was crying softly.

Explorers into infinity! And they were gone, to encounter—what?

4

THE WATCHERS

We spent the rest of that night in the little observation room on the upper story of Dr. Gryce's home; with him and with Fannie beside me I sat watching the vehicle's flight through the electro-telescope. It was not a high-powered instrument but it served. I could see the vehicle plainly as it passed through our atmosphere and out into space. A tiny blob with darker rectangles of windows.

Dr. Gryce sat with instruments, charts and his computation before him. Occasionally he would ask me for the vehicle's position; and I would give him the points and clock the time with all the accuracy of which I was capable. He seemed solemn, perturbed no longer; the scientist in him was all-absorbing. He said once with satisfaction, "Brett is competent— the boy hasn't varied a hair from my directions."

I knew that he and Brett had picked up the image of the girl and her assailants within a month past: and that Brett had accurate calculations which he could follow until able to capture the image on his own instruments.

"How long will it take them to get there?" I asked. "When will they be back? You said within a few days. How long?" Dr. Gryce looked up from his work with a faint smile. "There's no answer to that, Frank. Without a change of their time it might take them to reach that realm out there a thousand years or a million years—the vehicle's maximum velocity we do not know—that they are to find out."

EXPLORERS INTO INFINITY

BY Ray Cummings

Saturn with its rings was stupendously beautiful from our proximity.

"A million years—! And another million to come back!"

His smile broadened. "As we measure Time, yes. But they will change their Time-rate: the trip may seem to them only a few days."

"But," I persisted, "two million years of our Time! And we can not change our Time."

"No, Frank. But you speak thoughtlessly. Brett can return to any point in our Time he wishes. Not with exactitude—but, we hope,—within a few days. They will return here—within that Time we have agreed."

Frannie's face was very solemn though she said nothing; and I knew then that she was wondering if her brothers would be able to keep their promise.

Dr. Gryce rose from his chair. "I must adjust the aural ray— Brett may need it."

He had already explained this ray. A device similar to the familiar aurometer by which the aural power of the earth is measured. He had perfected an instrument for projecting into Space the invisible aura of the earth—projecting it in a tiny, very intense beam. An instrument for visualizing its characteristic bands was in the vehicle. They hoped that the ray might reach out into distant, interstellar Space; a flash of it crossing the sky as our earth rotated. And, coming back, Brett would see it, recognize it. A guide, as he came back from beyond all the universes strewn there throughout the magnitude of Space. If it could reach out there—if he saw it. My heart sank at the thoughts, doubts, which rushed upon me.

Dr. Gryce set his aural projector with its ray, invisible to the naked eye, flashing after the vehicle. Silently he returned to his seat.

"Can you see them? You can still see them, Frank?" Frannie turned to me with anxious face.

I could still see the vehicle. But faintly, for faster than any mail flyer it was winging its way outward. Mars—approaching its closest point to the earth now to bring a deluge of the Martian Mails—red Mars at midnight had been above us. The vehicle had gone that way; and now, visually beside the planet, they were sinking together in the western sky. The stars were paling with the coming dawn. The east flushed with it and presently I could see the vehicle no longer.

And as I turned from my instrument, I heard Dr. Gryce, "Why Frannie, girl! You're worn out. Come, it's dawn—they've vanished."

Little Frannie had fallen asleep.

5

THE RETURN

We did not sight the vehicle the next night; it had seemingly passed beyond range of my instrument. With the myrdo-scope we hoped to catch it, but could not. The night follow-ing was overcast with clouds. But we remained awake; Dr. Gryce seemed to feel that his sons might be returning. It was pathetic to me, observing him quietly slipping away from us at intervals to wander among the wreckage of his garden, gazing anxiously upward.

A week and still they had not come. What Dr. Gryce said to my Director I do not know; but he told me the Director was satisfied to have me remain away until my present business was finished I had determined as much for myself. Not all the Directors in the Service could have taken me away from here, with Brett and Martt unheard from.

Like a beacon day and night we made sure that our aural ray was flashing its beam. But would Brett see it?

Another week. Still no sign. Doubts, fears, terrors assailed us.

Were we watching, waiting futilely for what would never come? The thought was in my mind—and I knew it was in the minds of Dr. Gryce and Frannie—but never once did we voice it. Had Brett and Martt, perhaps, returned to our Past? With mechanism impaired, had they landed here in what we now called the Past—landed to find a wilderness of roaming savages? Or to find this little Space we now called a house and garden, a barren icy waste with men no more than beasts upon it? Or landed here in our Future? Ourselves dead, gone and forgotten? A great city here on this spot, perchance, with strange people and strange ways and nothing remaining of the loved ones they sought? Or were they lost and wandering in Space? Out there among myriad starry Universes hopeless to find our infinitesimal Solar System? Or lost perhaps in Time, wandering through the eons searching for the little centuries, years, days that identified their goal?

Or, again, perhaps they had safely reached that outer realm? Perhaps, once there, something had happened to prevent their return? In what we now call the Present, perhaps they were out there, transfixed, just as to our vision that strange girl and her strange assailants were transfixed—stricken of motion, with a passing of time to us insensible. Transfixed out there now, to take no more than a few breaths, to move a hand, no more, during all the span of our own tiny lives?

I was sitting early one evening near the midnight hour, alone with Frannie in the observation room. Dr. Gryce, in the room adjoining, had fallen asleep, worn by repressed anxiety and his now almost day and night vigil. We were talking in half-whispers; and abruptly Frannie voiced the fear that possessed us all.

"Oh. Frank, can't you see them? Please, you must! Oh, I'm afraid they're never coming back. Never—coming back."

It sounded so horrible. "Hush, Frannie. You mustn't say things like that." I put my arm around her, and suddenly like a child she flung herself to me; sobbed, and clung to me.

"Hush, Fannie. Don't cry—please don't cry. I'll look again. I might see them now. I'll try to."

I drew away from her; went back to my instrument. I had in mind to try the myrdoscope, but all our efforts with it during the two weeks past had been unavailing. It was a calm, clear evening. A broadly crescent moon was falling into the west. Mars was well above the eastern horizon; through the electro-telescope I looked that way. My circular field was empty. Frannie was checking her sobs, interested with hope renewed.

"Don't you see them. Frank?"

"No—Not yet—*Yes!* I see them! Frannie, I see them!"

From visually above the red planet, out of nothingness a huge shape suddenly materialized. It had not been there an instant before, it seemed for the space of a thought, a transparent ghost of the vehicle; solidifying until even before I had told Frannie, I was aware that I saw it there. The vehicle unmistakable.

"They've come. Frannie! I see them! Call your father. Dr. Gryce! They've come! They're safe!"

How my heart leaped to be able to say it! Frannie was calling; and Dr. Gryce, no more than half awake, repeating, "They've come? They're in sight? They're safe?"

This gentle old man, how full of thankfulness his heart must have been! He came stumbling into the room. "Where are they, Frank? You can see them, lad?"

I could see them indeed—plainly, for abruptly I realized that they were no farther than just beyond the earth's atmosphere. And I could see also the conventional vane flying at horizontal above the vehicle's tower to denote that all was well within. They had come. They were safe.

They landed in the garden. Like a wafting feather the vehicle floated down under Brett's skilled guidance. It was of a size seemingly identical with the one it had upon departure, but evidence of its trip was everywhere visible. Its gleaming milk-white color was dulled. Its sides were pitted and scarred—the metal burned. A lower corner seemed fused into a shapeless lump.

The door slid open as we crowded forward. My heart was pounding. A sudden, irrelevant thought leaped to me—a thought, hope, that they might have brought back with them that strangely beautiful girl they had gone to rescue. A thought abruptly, fiercely poignant—yet with it a consciousness of its whimsicality that I—Frank Elgon—who loved Frannie Gryce, should be possessed of such incongruous desire.

The door was open. Brett and Martt—queerly garbed to seem almost strangers—were crowding there, with no one else behind them. But already I had forgotten the girl. Frannie's glad cries of welcome rang out; and Dr. Gryce's tremulous greeting; and I heard my own voice, strangely calm, "Well! Brett—Martt—you got back safely, didn't you? I'm so glad— we're all so glad!"

6

THE FLIGHT INTO TIME, SIZE AND SPACE

They seemed not tired, but undoubtedly they were hungry, famished; and before they would say a word of those strange things we knew they had to tell, they made us feed them. "Regular food," as Martt laughingly called it. "By the code! We've eaten for months weird things supposed to be edible. My digestion is ruined."

Months! They had been gone two weeks and two days into a realm where those little sixteen days were no more than a tiny fraction of a second! Yet they spoke of months! It was very strange.

"Frannie! *Don't* ask me that again." Martt affectionately tweaked her chin. "We found her, I tell you. Wait till we've had supper—you'll hear."

They ate with the relish of those long deprived of accustomed food; and as we sat with them, forbearing to ask the eager questions flooding us, again I had that impression of the strangeness which had come to them. It was not only their manner of dress, though that of itself was extraordinary. They wore shirts of a colored cloth with a high rolling collar in front, low and open in back. Short trousers that were queerly wide and flapping at the knee, stockings that seemed of a soft gray leather and long-pointed shoes of a material I could not name. Over the shirt a short jacket, wide-shouldered and with sleeves that puffed and flared; and a skirt to it at the waist which rolled upward. Their hats—which Frannie rescued from the vehicle—

were solidly wooden of aspect, with low circular crowns and triangular stiff brims.

The garb seemed grotesque; yet they took it so as a matter of course when once we ceased our comments—and they were so easy in it, so unconscious of it that abruptly I realized it was my own viewpoint that held the strangeness. Between them, also, there was a difference of aspect—a rationality to their characters. The colors of their garments materially differed. Brett's clothes were more sober—less vivid, less extreme. His shirt was a somber brown; Martt's was a glaring green. Martt's jacket had additional bangles fastened to its cloth, it rolled higher in the skirt; tassels depended from his elbows longer than those Brett wore, his jacket sleeves were fuller; his trousers flared more, and were a more brilliant hue. But I will say that when after a time I became in a measure accustomed to his looks, Martt was very handsome; and he carried himself with a sort of swinging, debonair grace and swagger wholly attractive.

They were strangers to us in their mode of dress; no one regarding them could have named a nation of earth or any of the habited planets from which they might have come. Yet the strangeness went deeper than their clothes. They seemed older. A vague aspect of command seemed upon them—especially did it envelop Brett, like an aura sensed but not seen. Martt's old jocularity was unchanged; no dignity, no reservation, no aloofness with us had been added to the new swagger. Yet beneath his laughter there seemed always a hidden solemnity. And then I saw it all—this subtle strangeness that clung to them—I saw it lurking in their eyes. Memories mirrored there; memories of things no man had seen and felt before. Eyes— and more especially Brett's eyes—which had seen, perhaps, too much.

It was Brett who began their narrative; began it with the slow, careful, precise phrasing of the scientist anxious to avoid error of memory; to be exact of every fact and detail. On his lap he held a book of notes, and another book of the many dial recordings. He consulted it.

"Our recorded time of starting was four minutes past midnight. Sixteen days ago, wasn't it, Father? Sixteen!"

He gave a queer laugh but did not comment upon his thoughts. "I had determined to start slowly. Martt would have rushed us, but I thought that caution was best until we were quite sure of the workings of these mechanisms new to us.

"I did not record our passing above the earth's atmosphere. But the vehicle was inordinately hot from the friction of our passage. Perhaps I took it too fast—at all events we did not bother with refrigeration since in Space we would so soon need the heaters. We sat sweltering at the main instrument table with the dials before us.

"I think, Father, that I followed your instructions carefully. The dials were all set and operating. The size dials stood motionless at unit 1. Our relative Time-dials were motionless at the original unit of earth Time; and the earth dial-chronometers ticked off the passing of your seconds and minutes. On the Space dials—when first I chanced to notice them—we had gone some 900 miles. Our velocity then had picked up to 1,500 miles an hour and was swiftly accelerating. The Time was 1 a.m.

"It is slow getting through the atmosphere, but now we were fairly on our way. As you suggested, Father, I was heading just a point off Mars where I could hold Jupiter and Saturn almost in a line ahead of us. They were all there visible through our floor window—we had turned over and were falling toward them. I was using a fraction only of the earth's repulsion, and holding steady with the selective attraction of Mars and the star-field behind it."

"We saw your aural ray," Martt put in. He was earnestly intent upon Brett's narrative. "We saw it—I saw it—through the spectrometer. The swing of it was apparent even at that near distance. And we saw the Martian Mail coming in—they landed in Eurasia that night, I suppose. Say, they move in a hurry, don't they? And stop in a hurry when they get down close."

Brett went on: "We were still within the lower cone of the earth's shadow. But presently we emerged and came into the sunlight. The brilliant blackness of Space; and the cold by now had penetrated so that very soon we were glad enough to use the heaters.

"You know the details of a Martian voyage, Father. And you, Frank? This was no different except that having no necessity of stopping I reached a greater velocity than they generally obtain. A forty-hour trip, isn't it, Frank?"

"There's nearly always one of the minimum distance trips at about that," I answered. "But you had some sixty million miles for yours. That's a lot longer than a minimum distance."

He nodded. "Yes. We came abreast of Mars—I suppose about a million miles away. Our Space-dials showed about sixty-two million miles traveled. We had been gone from you thirty-nine hours. Our average velocity had been something over a million and a half miles an hour, and with steadily increasing acceleration had reached then nearly three million an hour.

"That was as quick a trip as you anticipated, Father? But even so, we found it irksome. We alternated at the instrument board. Martt prepared most of the meals—beyond that and sleeping there was little to do. Except to watch for asteroids; but the mails have reported the region through there remarkably free of them this season. We saw none inside the Martian orbit closer than a million miles, which to such a low velocity as ours held no danger."

Dr. Gryce asked, "The air purifiers. Brett? You had no trouble?"

"No. Or very little, except just at first with the chlorate of potassium. I was telling you about passing Mars. We saw it rising slowly past us—saw it through a side window. A huge crescent, the sunlight on half its disk, but even the unlighted portion was plainly outlined. Above us was the thin crescent earth, with the sun behind it. The tongues of flame in the sun's envelope were plainer than I had ever seen them. We were falling away from the earth and sun, into the inky blackness of Space with its blazing white stars.

"During all this first portion of the trip we were eager to get more quickly advanced. Beyond Neptune's orbit, with the Solar System once behind us, we would feel like explorers, even though Nogar—he holds the record, doesn't he?—went once 27,000 million miles out."

Dr. Gryce put in: "His record was 27,600 million miles from our sun. At nearly five million miles an hour, which was his maximum velocity obtainable, that trip for the full return passage consumed—I think the total time was 461 days."

Brett went on. "That was the record. But even to go a single light-year at that velocity would have taken Nogar around 84 years just going out a little light-year of distance, to say nothing of getting back! And we had so many thousands of light-years to travel even to get beyond the stars. It seemed stupendous—impossible."

"Naturally," said Dr. Gryce. "Impossible, of course, had you held to that size." They were directing their explanations at me. I nodded. "But you didn't stay that size?" I suggested.

"No, of course not," said Brett. "But for a time, we did—I was cautious from Mars to Jupiter, Father. Nogar plunged right through the asteroid region there—plunged through at nearly his five million miles an hour velocity. I held down to three million. We kept a close watch, though Martt had a somewhat terrifying experience. Tell them, Martt."

Martt flushed a trifle. "It wasn't my fault—at least I didn't think so. At a velocity like that the space there between the orbits of Mars and Jupiter is horribly crowded. Brett was asleep. I sat by the instrument table staring down into the floor window at the black firmament into which we were dropping. You people take a voyage like this as a matter of course—but it was my first time off earth, and the beauty of it—of the heavens—well, I tell you it impressed me. The black firmament—those blazing constellations beneath us—the full moon of Jupiter every moment growing larger like a white round lamp down there.

"Well, anyway, perhaps, I was lost in thoughts of it—when leaping up out of the blackness came a great round silver disk. A hundred times the size of our full moon. Then a thousand. It was below me, but off to our side. It swept past, so close I could see its barren, rocky surface—a range of desolate gray mountains; and, I could see, too, its rotation, like a ball tossed into the air slowly rotating. Before I could think to do anything— even to make a move—the asteroid went past, out of my field as I looked through the floor window. For a moment I saw it rising past a side window and then it was above us—gone completely beyond my sight in a moment or two. I want to tell you I was frightened—I called Brett down at once."

Brett laughed. "I found him white, shaking like a tower-trembler. If a collision had really threatened, he could have thrown the main Time-Switch. Thrown us suddenly into the asteroid's past or future—I had told him that—but when the danger came, he never thought of it."

"I never did," Martt confessed.

"How close did the asteroid pass?" I asked. "I saw one once, on a Martian trip—"

"I suppose we passed it at a distance of some three thousand miles," Brett answered. "But at three million miles an hour we were traveling that distance in three or four seconds. It was a narrow escape. The asteroid's attraction, had drawn us aside from our course—but I soon rectified that."

"I meant to explain about attraction a moment ago, Frank," Dr. Gryce interrupted. "The attraction of the vehicle on our planets is why Brett could not yet increase his size. Jupiter and Saturn were pulling the vehicle onward, and in direct proportion to the mass, of course, the vehicle was pulling at them. An infinitesimal pull—but had Brett increased its size materially while still close to our planets—the vehicle would have been a seriously disturbing element. I did not want that. Indeed, with any great size-increase, the vehicle moving out there would have thrown our whole system into chaos."

Brett said, "I was careful to obey you, Father. We were safely beyond Saturn—and Uranus and Neptune were on the other side of the sun—before I even touched the size switch. From the orbit of Mars to that of Jupiter there are some 334 million miles between the points we crossed. We were about 112 hours making the voyage. I kept us well away—some ten million miles. But the planet was a beautiful sight, assuming every phase from full to crescent as we passed. You have never been so close, Father? Nor you Frank?"

"Nor I," spoke up Frannie. She said it in a whimsical fashion of pathos, as though to make us all realize that she had been neglected.

Brett laughed affectionately. "No, nor you, little sister. Well, it's a beautiful sight. You can see it similarly in the telescope, but somehow, at the same visual distance the naked eye shows it indefinably different. A beautiful silver disk with the broad dark bands upon it and the red spot glowing like a lantern in its lower hemisphere.

"Our velocity was slackened for a time as we passed Jupiter, since I had to lose its great attractive force and turn a neutral side to it. But once by it, with it blazing as a gigantic thin crescent above us, I used a full power of its repulsion. We gained velocity rapidly. With the region of minor planets passed I had no fear of using all the velocity we could obtain. I think Nogar was unskillful in the handling of his vehicle; at all events, before we reached the neighborhood of Saturn, we had attained a velocity of seven and a half million miles an hour. It was the greatest velocity we reached."

"But," I exclaimed, "but Brett, at seven and one-half million miles an hour, in your whole life-time—whether you changed your Time-rate or not, you would have to live those hours—in a whole life-time at that velocity you wouldn't get one-quarter of the distance even to the nearest star!"

"No," he agreed. "But I began using the size-change after we passed Saturn—"

I interrupted again. "I've been wondering about that—I don't quite see—"

"I'll make it clear to you, Frank, in a moment," Dr. Gryce put in. "Go on, Brett."

"We were well past Saturn before I changed our size at all. Our average velocity along there was six million miles an hour—it was a run of about seventy-five hours. We would have been—even at our maximum of seven and one-half million miles an hour—more than another 240 hours getting past

Neptune's orbit. It was too tedious. We determined, since Uranus and Neptune were in other parts of their orbits—far on the other side of our sun—I decided once we were well beyond Saturn we would start our increase of size. We were seventy million miles beyond Saturn, with nothing of importance ahead of us but the distant stars when I determined to start the change. The space there was comparatively deserted—a few asteroids—sometimes we could go nearly an hour without even sighting one.

"With Martt beside me we were both a little timid about it, naturally—I threw over the switch and started our growth."

He paused for the length of a breath. "It was extraordinary—all our experience of the voyage from that moment was extraordinary. I hardly know how to begin tell you...."

Dr. Gryce interrupted. "Just a minute, Brett—I want to make absolutely clear to Frank the principles involved in this change of size in relation to velocity."

"May I ask a question first?" I hazarded.

"All you like," said Brett.

"I'm wondering why in your normal size you could attain no greater velocity than seven and one half million miles an hour. Theoretically, you know, a freely falling body will accelerate to infinity. And with repulsion added—a body, not only falling, but being *pushed* downward—"

Frannie said "Nogar found his approximate limit at five million—"

"Our limitations were similar to his," Martt put in.

"I know," I said. "I remember in the public newscasting they said—"

"We found the same conditions," Brett put it. "Our vehicle—any vehicle traveling in outer Space—is not strictly a freely falling body. For low velocities—the general voyaging from here to Mercury, Venus or Mars—Space may almost be considered a vacuum. But it is not a vacuum as we know. The imponderable, widely separated atoms of the ether—to use the ancient word—begin to be a factor at velocities over three million miles an hour. The drag became increasingly noticeable—"

"And the heat of the friction warmed us up," Martt put in. "At six million miles an hour we were hot let me tell you. Sweltering even with the full refrigeration units going."

"That friction held us to seven and one-half million as our limit," Brett added. "Anything else, Frank?"

"Yes I was wondering about our aural ray here. Could you still see it?"

"Oh yes. Our sun of the Solar System had dwindled—small, but white and brilliant. With the naked eye the little star which was our earth showed very faint but distinguishable. With the aurometer—even using its spreading field of vision so that it embraced all that portion of the sky—we could see your beam sweeping slowly across the field as the earth rotated."

"And the myrdoscope?" I suggested. "Hadn't you tried again to locate the image of that girl?" My heart thumped as I said it.

He nodded. "Beyond Jupiter, when the long hours of inactivity hung on us, I spent many of them, searching ahead of us with the myrdoscope. At last I picked up the image of the girl—held it for a few moments."

"There was no change?" Dr. Gryce said eagerly.

"No. The little distance we had traveled made no change—in fact, my smaller instrument, Father, showed it rather less clearly."

"I mean no change in the girl's attitude," Dr. Gryce insisted. "No change in the attacking giant or those grinning little dwarfs at the girl's ankle?"

"None. But she was aware of them. On her face was stark terror—as we had seen it from here, Father, a month before. I noticed that the giant's forward step had nearly been completed—and the climbing dwarf was holding tightly to her sandal cord."

Brett gazed at me inquiringly but I shook my head. "That's all I have to ask," I said. "Go ahead, Brett. You were telling us about how you started the size-change—"

Dr. Gryce put in. "I think you had best proceed, Brett. And then if there is anything Frank does not understand, we can stop and make it clear."

He nodded, but for a moment he hesitated. "I flung over the switch to start our growth," he said slowly. "It was the beginning of all those strangely weird experiences which followed now one upon the other. Frightening at first...."

He paused briefly, then went on; "Our first sensation was one of shock—a reeling of the senses. But it was not severe—it passed almost at once. We found ourselves clinging there to the instrument table. To me the room seemed swaying dizzily. My forehead was damp with cold moisture; a nausea possessed me. I was oppressed; the air of the room was heavy to breathe."

"The air was snapping with the current," said Martt. "I could see it, and feel it tingling against my face. And it was heavy to breathe, as Brett says."

Brett resumed: "But we felt better after a moment. I saw the change first on the dials. The pointer of the lowest unit dial of the size series was slowly but visibly moving. I watched as it crept from 1 to 2. We had doubled in size, I gazed about the room. It was unchanged; and now as my body rapidly adjusted itself to the new conditions, I began to feel almost normal. Except a queer whirring in my head, and the nausea which persisted for perhaps an hour, I felt no evidence of the growth. The room, the vehicle was untrembling. No slightest evidence within the vehicle of the size-change going on—except the creeping pointer of the lowest dial. It was moving faster; it had reached 10. The pointer of the dial beside it—registering in units of a hundred—now seemed stirring."

Brett gazed at us earnestly. "I want to make myself absolutely clear. We were then—I suppose a minute or so had elapsed— we were ten times our original size—"

"Much faster than the vehicle grew in the garden," I exclaimed.

"Yes. I had chanced the possibility of severe shock and thrown the lever at once to a quarter strength. Martt and Frannie, in the garden, had put it on only to the one-hundredth part of its power. At all intensities, the growth, you understand, constantly accelerates. At unit 10, which we reached in possibly the first minute, we were ten times our starting size—that is, for earth measurements, our vehicle from base to tower-top was then one-tenth of a mile. But soon the pointer had passed 50. And then 100—and the pointer of the hundred-unit dial had crept to 1.

"With recovered normality of senses we had gone to the windows. I want you to visualize first what always before we had seen. An ink black void everywhere surrounding us, in the center of which seeming we hung motionless. The brilliant firmament of stars, freed from distortion of earth's atmosphere glittering, blazing like great diamonds. Pure white, blue-white, or tinged with yellow and red. The whole extent of the heavens swarming with them. The huge, spiral nebulous masses fleecy white, with tiny points of blazing white fire in them. And behind them all that distant ring of seeming star-dust— immeasurably distant yet glowing a silver veil, which in the ancient books they called the 'Milky Way.'

"Near at hand, above us were the tiny planets of our Solar System. The sun, only a pale white disk from out here near Saturn; the earth a star very faint; red Mars, a tiny reddish dot. But Jupiter was brilliant; and Saturn from our proximity was stupendously beautiful. The globe itself—a great silver disk, with the sunlight to make a narrow portion of it into a blazing crescent. The darkened areas of the globe, even on the shadowed portion, were plain almost as the bands of Jupiter. And Saturn's rings! Concentric rings—the inner one a trifle darker—opened into a narrow angle—a glowing silver band like a broad hat-brim encircling the planet—a hat-brim over 37,000 miles broad.

"This we saw, with ourselves of unchanging size. But now we were growing. The change was at first apparent only in the aspect of Saturn—since it was closest to us. The planet seemed to become a little smaller—shrinking and creeping toward us. A contraction of its size—and as though the space between us were diminishing. Yet—as a seeming paradox—the visual diameter of the globe and the rings remained almost the same.

"It is difficult to describe. We seemed moving closer to Saturn, yet in no sense was there any apparent motion. The effect— the result—of seeming motion—not the motion itself. Martt presently went back to watch the dials. He called out to me when we had reached unit 1,000. A thousand times our original size—the vehicle now ten miles in earthly height. The change had now affected very slightly the entire firmament. Everywhere a seeming contraction—not so much in the aspect of the blazing star-points, but in the black void of Space itself. As though the void were smaller—contracted so that everything in it were of necessity a little nearer to us. But it was as yet barely noticeable. I might even have thought it a psychological co-action with the change in Saturn's aspect—a change unmistakable.

"Saturn, as we grew, had been seemingly smaller and coming visually nearer to us. Yet our velocity away from it was—in our original size—seven and one-half million miles an hour. Can I make you realize that the effect of *both* motions was apparent? It was as though we were moving forward to lengthen a dwindling distance, with Saturn following after us simultaneously to shorten it.

"It was at the thousand unit point—ourselves then ten miles of earthly height—that I shut off the size-switch. Of visual diameter, Saturn had really not altered materially."

Brett stopped as though carefully to choose his words. "I'm striving to give you a clear picture. A distant object of great size may appear of the same diameter as something smaller and closer. But you can generally tell which is which. There is a difference of aspect—impossible to describe, but readily seen. Saturn was like that—the change in the planet was like a progressive change from the one condition to the other. It had appeared large and distant; it changed, to be smaller and closer. Just before I shut off the size-switch, when our rate of growth had become comparatively rapid, Saturn took on other motions—I'll tell you about them in a moment.

"Do I make myself clear? I want to…. With our growth checked, there was at once a striking, visual result. We seemed receding from Saturn so fast that its apparent diameter dwindled very rapidly—a normal dwindling of rapidly added distance. Presently it was a mere star—then a pin-point of light. Then it was vanished. Our other planets of the Solar System had preceded Saturn into invisibility. Then our sun itself became so faint a star that I lost it. We were beyond the

Solar System—itself wholly lost to the naked eye among the great star-clusters enveloping it."

"Wait," I exclaimed. "There is so much I want to ask you, Brett."

Frannie interposed timidly: "Did you say, Brett, that on earth the vehicle then would have been ten miles in height?"

"Yes," he agreed.

She commented, "Then your relative Time-dials must have been visibly moving—"

Dr. Gryce hastily interrupted: "The practical workings of the inherent Time-change I want Brett to explain carefully. You did not move the vehicle in Time, did you, Brett?"

"No sir. Not then."

I must have looked puzzled, for Dr. Gryce added: "We mean, Frank, that the vehicle could have traveled in Time—in earth-Time, for instance, to go into our past or our future. Brett had not done that. But immediately the vehicle started a size-change, you understand, there automatically began a Time-change inherent to that growth. Normal to it, let me say."

"Oh, yes," I nodded. "I remember you explained that. In relation to its size—"

"I'll put it this way," Dr. Gryce went on. "That girl out there is moving through Time at a definite rate. Let us say a year of our Time would he measured as a second of hers."

"Less than that," Martt interjected.

"Yes lad, I know. But those rough figures will serve for the present comparison." He turned back to me. "Keep that in mind, Frank. Now conceive Brett and Martt changing progressively upward in size, from what they are here on earth, to a size normal to that girl and the realm she lives in. A corresponding Time-change must take place. At every point of the voyage in Time and size, the relative values must agree; the vehicle's Time-rate always must be in inverse proportion to its position in size."

I nodded. "I think I understand. You mean that when in size the vehicle had progressed half-way from our size to the girl's, that then the vehicle's normal Time-rate would be half-way between, our Time and hers?"

"Exactly, Frank."

"At this ten-mile size what percentage of the size-journey had been made?" I asked. I smiled. "I'm trying to imagine how large that girl may be."

Brett said quickly, "I'll tell you that later. It was some distance farther on before I could calculate such relative values even as approximations."

Frannie said, "At that point, Brett, the vehicle began speeding into the earth's future, didn't it?"

Dr. Gryce exclaimed: "Child, that will only lead us into philosophical discussion. Beyond the realm of mathematics—"

"I don't think so, Father," Brett said quietly. "I would say that since everything—Size, Time and Space—is relative, depending wholly on the viewpoint of the observer—that Frannie's question is simple enough. To me as observer—to my consciousness there in the vehicle—every given instant was the Present. The earth was out there in Space, revolving about its sun; rotating on its axis—its movements to my consciousness *faster* than before. To me it was the Present. The earth was there. I saw it through the electro-telescope. I also saw your aural ray through the aurometer. The ray swept the sky with a rapid sweep since to my altered Time-rate the earth was rotating faster. But every given instant was my Present.

"However, compare my consciousness to yours on earth. The earth—rotating faster relative to me—had while I watched there, made, let us say, a full rotation in that first five minutes of my vigil. Relative to me—it was the earth's future Time. I was gazing upon earth in its *tomorrow*. So I think that I was, as Fannie said, speeding into the earth's future"

Frannie was triumphant. Dr. Gryce said smilingly, "You put it clearly, Brett. But it's a philosophical and metaphysical viewpoint nevertheless. You spoke of Saturn's having another apparent motion near the end of your size-change?"

"Yes," said Brett, "As our Time-rate became materially slower, the speeding up of all the motions inherent to the planets grew visible. Saturn's rotation on its axis became readily visible through the telescope. And the globe began very slowly shifting sidewise—at nearly right angles to our course—the visual result of the intensification of its orbital movement.... You were going to ask a question, Frank, a moment ago?"

I had not forgotten it. "You were telling us, Brett, how you stopped your growth at the ten-mile size. Almost immediately, you said, Saturn receded into an invisibility of distance. The entire Solar System vanished into distance, You had been traveling only seven and one-half million miles an hour before changing size It was the new velocity I wanted to ask about. The whole question of velocity relative to size."

"Relative!" Brett exclaimed. "That's the keynote to it, Frank. Two differing viewpoints, always. Keep them both in mind—the viewpoint of earth-size, and the viewpoint of the vehicle-size. I'll try and explain it now. Once clear to you, our whole experience will clarify to your understanding. Conceive, from your external viewpoint of earth, the vehicle out there in Space dropping with a velocity of seven and one-half million miles an hour. That was its maximum, owing to the ether-friction. It started to increase in size. Hence its mass grew in proportion directly as the cube. As the mass grew greater, the atoms of the ether became of themselves relatively smaller, less ponderable, less capable of exerting their frictional drag.

"This should be very clear to you, Frank. In a vacuum, a feather and a bit of lead fall at equal rates. The mass—the weight—has nothing to do with it. But in air—where there is a friction the heavier object falls faster. The vehicle was like that. Its mass, so enormously increased, gave it a greatly increased maximum velocity. It picked up velocity rapidly with its growth. The formulas involved are intricate—I need only say that after forty-nine minutes of traveling at the ten-mile size, we had again reached maximum. It was about 200 million miles a minute."

"A minute!" I exclaimed.

"Yes. That is 12,000 million miles an hour, as against seven and one-half million. The vehicle's length, breadth and width had each increased to a thousand times their former size. Its mass was the product of the three—hence one thousand million times greater.

"These are all approximate to the actual figures, you understand. Round numbers are less confusing. Our resultant velocity, however, was 200 million miles a minute, at the end of the first hour. We were well beyond the Solar System by then."

Frannie asked, "Brett, why didn't Saturn appear to recede until after you had stopped your growth?"

"That was merely optical, Frannie. Our velocity away from Saturn was steadily increasing. But with our increasing size, the space seemed dwindling—as though Saturn were following after us. With the growth cheeked there was a visual reaction—an apparent leaping away. It was merely optical. Anything else?"

"I'd like to know," I said, "the relation of your Time in the vehicle at the ten-mile size—its relation to our earth-Time."

"The proportion of one to one thousand," he answered readily. "Seven seconds to me, then, was about two hours on earth. Could I have seen the earth when I reached that maximum, it would have made a complete rotation on its axis—a day of yours—in a minute and twenty-four seconds to me.

"It's all clear, isn't it? Suppose I go back to the details of our trip? With ten miles of earthly size, at a velocity of 200 million miles a minute we were dropping into the black void of Space. The Solar System was lost presently, even to telescopic vision but with the naked eye the firmament of stars was very little changed. I searched with the myrdoscope for the image of the girl, but did not chance to pick it up. We were hot again within the vehicle from the ether-friction—as hot as we had been before.

"Beneath us, in the star-field for which I was heading, was Alpha Centauri. It is, as you know, one of the very closest stars to our Solar System—to our earth. In miles, roughly some 25,000,000,000,000. Four and a third light-years of distance, 4.35 light-years to be exact. At 200 million miles a minute we would have been some eighty-eight days getting there."

"I couldn't have stood a trip so long," Martt exclaimed. "I told him we'd have to increase our size again. Nearly three months to get to the nearest star—with others a thousand times farther on!"

"There was no reason for us to stay so small," Brett agreed. "Out there, with the Solar System so far away, I had no fear of disturbing it."

Again I interrupted. "Brett, the vehicle's velocity was then much greater than the velocity of light—"

"About eighteen times greater."

"It seems inconceivable," I added. "Impossible for any tangible entity in Space to attain such velocity."

"Ah, but Frank, that's where you're using the wrong viewpoint," Dr. Gryce exclaimed warmly. "You're still imagining yourself an observer on earth. But take the viewpoint of the vehicle. Space was proportionately smaller than before. Brett gives you the earth-size figures in order to avoid confusion. From the vehicle's enlarged viewpoint, Brett, what was its comparative velocity?"

"About twelve million miles an hour," Brett said. "As against a former seven and one-half million. Not so great a change, Frank?"

"No," I admitted. "But—"

"But you can not quite grasp how the two velocities can be the same? Existing simultaneously in the same vehicle, only with a differing view-point?"

I think that was my trouble. I nodded, and he said at once, "To the larger viewpoint, Frank, the Space had diminished a thousand times, to make a thousand miles become as one mile. Not an *actual* change—a relative change only. But twelve million miles an hour, with distance diminished one thousand times, is the same as twelve thousand million miles an hour with the distance factor unaltered. You see that, of course. Or consider the relative Time-values. The vehicle's Time was seven seconds to about two hours. The exact figures were one to one-thousand. In the vehicle we lived a thousand earth-seconds in one. Applied, then, to the two viewpoints of velocity, it gives identical results for the distance traveled. Whatever the factors involved—the earth-Time; the vehicle-Time; the Space relative to the vehicle; or to the earth; and the velocity, relative either to the vehicle-size or earth-size—the result must be mathematically the same. You see? And, Frank, in describing the progressive size-changes into which we now plunged, I shall give you always Space with earth-standard and our velocity from the viewpoint of earth. It reached tremendous figures; but you are to remember always that of actuality they must be divided by the relative size factor. They were never greater than you would have expected the vehicle to obtain.

"I was saying that we were headed for Alpha Centauri. Again we started the growth. I threw the switch to its fullest intensity. Martt stayed to watch the dials; I sat on the floor, gazing down through the window at the star-field spread out beneath me. When my head had cleared from the shock of starting the growth, I sat absorbed in watching. Soon visible movements appeared. The star-drifts began to be apparent. And we were going toward these stars; the apparent shortening Space, added to our increasing relative velocity, made their approach visible. In the field to the sides of us, the stars were shifting upward. Those in front were spreading apart with a movement very slow but perceptible as we dropped toward them.

"I do not know how long I sat there; Martt occasionally would call to me from his post at the dials, but I hardly heard him. Alpha Centauri presently came rushing forward. As you know, it is a binary—twin stars a few hundred million miles apart, its components revolving about each other with a period of eighty-one years. It had been one blazing white point of light. Then it separated into two. They stayed visually small, for they were dwindling before the vehicle's growth; but they came rushing toward us. Soon I could see them separated by a narrow black ribbon of the void; and could see them revolving one about the other."

"An eighty-one-year period, and you could see it!" I exclaimed.

"Yes—a very slow movement, but I could see it. I would have passed between them—the ribbon of Space there was widening rapidly, the stars themselves had become great, blazing white-hot suns. But I was afraid of the heat; I altered our course to present a slightly repellent side. The firmament turned partly over. The two stars swung up past our side window; in visual diameter larger than our earthly sun—they mounted upward, closed in above us, drew together to form one; a sun at first then a brilliant star; then faint, until with the naked eye I lost it.

"Beneath us, the star-field in front was rushing upward much faster now. The constellations opening; the stars shifting—everywhere was movement—strange movement, unnatural, fantastic. I confess, Father, that I was injudicious. Martt was absorbed, fascinated in watching the dials, and when occasionally he would call to me, I told him everything was all right."

"I didn't know what was going on," said Martt. "You told me to sit there and I sat there."

"Of course you didn't know what was going on," Brett smiled. "But I did, and I think for a time I lost my wits. The stars were thick and close around us. The nebulae were opened into individual points of fire. Everywhere was movement, unreal. Stars rotating visibly; binaries shifting about each other; other stars shifting about each other; other stars seeming to enlarge in size, or to diminish, to swing this way or that with all the optical vagaries of our velocity, our changing Time and Size; and always those of the star-field in front—beneath us—spreading to the sides, rushing past our windows, closing in above us and fading into invisibility.

"A myriad universes in fantastic motion. And suddenly I realized that these giant suns were very close to us, and very small! Some I had recognized—blazing globes 100 million miles and more in diameter, and thought myself ten times that far from them. But it was not so. I stared at a giant globe 100 million miles in diameter, and with my viewpoint suddenly changed I saw that it was no more than a tiny glowing meteor, sweeping past a few miles away!"

"All this star-field, little balls, rolling close upon us. A miracle that none hit us, though some time before, I had had the wit to call to Martt to make all the faces repellent. By inertia only, we plunged onward, repelling what lay in our path.

"I saw a wandering asteroid—a few hundred miles perhaps in diameter. It was whirling on its axis like a ball thrown into the air. A whimsical humor—a madness perhaps—had descended upon me. There was nothing but the asteroid momentarily close before us, and I called to Martt to throw attraction into the bottom of the vehicle. The asteroid came rushing. But shrinking—shrinking until I laughed aloud to see it dwindle to a ball I could have held in my hand; and dwindle further until impotently it struck the floor window with a tiny point of fire from its fusing rock and metal. A burning cinder which scarce would have hurt me had I caught it in my naked hands.

"**How long** my mood of ironic madness may have lasted I can not say. I barely noticed our actual entry into the Galactic Plane. Enormous suns whirling past, now relatively not many times bigger than the vehicle itself. Others, distant a mile or so—or a billion miles if you want the other viewpoint—with their magnified drift making them dart crazily past. I gave no heed to passing time; I remember only that at last the star-field beneath us was thinning out. Stray clusters—a myriad glowing little balls hurled aside by our rush. But there were visibly less and less of them, until, quite suddenly, I realized that unbroken inky darkness lay ahead. And to the sides and above us, the star clusters, nebulae; swirling like silver mist— it was all fading. Winking little points up there behind us— winking and vanishing.

"We were in blackness unbroken. Dropping into a void of blackness with velocity inconceivable. Suddenly I was frightened. Stiff from so long upon the floor, I rose and hurried to Martt. We shut off the size-switch; made all the faces repellent. But there was nothing to repel; nothing to stop our downward rush into that blackness. It seemed all at once a blackness pregnant with unseen things of fearsome aspect.... The size-dials showed us to be near unit 50,000,000. Fifty million times our original size! The vehicle 500,000 miles high!

"The relative Time-dials—showing relative earth-Time—were whirling. Our Time in the vehicle was less than a single second to a year on earth. My mind leaped back to you. Every second we lived there in the vehicle you here on earth were living more than a year. A century of yours was little more than a minute to us. The earth's future, whirling on a thousand years while Martt and I sat there confused at the instrument table. A tiny little earth, spinning like a top upon its axis, flashing around its tiny sun with a complete revolution every second!

"The velocity indicators, as well were in rapid motion. The indicator of the miles-per-hour unit was an indistinguishable blur. And miles per minute—and per second—we could read none of them, so fast were they moving. The light-year distance pointers were in motion. We were piling up light-years of distance every moment. The total stood—as momentarily I read it—at between eleven and twelve thousand light-years of total distance traveled. Light speeding at 186,000 miles a second must go a year to make a light-year unit of distance. And we had gone nearly 12,000 light-years! I read our present velocity on the light-years velocity-dial. It was 3480 light-years per hour! And still rapidly accelerating!

"The panic of fear possessed us at the strangeness of it all—at that void of blackness—soundlessness—into which we were plunging; and even our plunge unmarked by the faintest trembling of the vehicle. A panic. I started to use the aurometer to search for your ray. Absurd! The absurdity of it made me laugh hysterically. Your ray had been extinguished thousands of years in my past. I tried the myrdoscope—to locate the image of the girl—to verify our direction, for abruptly I realized I had, in that empty black void, nothing by which I might locate our position.

"The myrdoscope was inoperative! I could not locate the girl-image—nor anything else. I tried with the electro-telescope at its greatest power—tried frantically to pick up some star-image behind us. I could not. I did not think they were as yet beyond its range—it merely had gone dead. The current in it would not hum. It was dead like the myrdoscope. We wondered then if our dials were working accurately. In our panic we doubted everything. And knew, with a stark terror upon us—knew that we were lost. Lost perhaps in Size and Time. And lost in black Space, empty, soundless, unfathomable!"

7

"A SINGLE STARLIT NIGHT—AN ETERNITY"

Brett had momentarily paused in his narrative, but when we would have plied him with questions he waved us aside.

"Let us finish first. The panic that was upon us with this knowledge—belief—that we were lost out there in Time and Size and Space did not last long, for we fought against it. And presently we were calmer—able to reason. Our size-dials were at rest—we had shut off the switch. By earth standards the vehicle was 500,000 miles in height. Our relative Time was a century of yours, to a little more than a minute of ours. Some 8,000 years into your earth-future had already piled up on the earth standard Time-dial—and we were adding one hundred years to it almost every minute. Our velocity had reached a maximum of 3480 light-years per hour—and we were 12,000 light-years from earth. The velocity was now lessening a trifle; it dropped nearly to an even 3,000. With unchanging size now, with nothing near us to repel or attract, the ether friction overcame inertia to reach a balance of forces.

"We conquered our fear—began to reason what we should do. It was of course futile to look for your aural ray. It had been extinguished thousands of years. We wanted to go on to our destination, and it was the non-operation of the myrdoscope which worried and puzzled us…. I was sure, Father, that up to this point in the voyage I had made no serious error of direction. The image of the girl should have been before us. But the myrdoscope would not work."

"The Time—" I suggested.

"Ah, no, Frank! We had progressed very little into the Time of that girl's life. She should still have been reclining there on the bank; or at least the bank itself should have been there. We puzzled over what could be the trouble with the myrdoscope. We found the trouble—"

"I found it," said Martt eagerly.

Brett nodded. "Yes, it was Martt who reasoned it out. A curious explanation—and one, I think, which involves the greatest of all the issues we had encountered. The myrdoscope would not operate for a very big, but very simple reason. You would think to find the answer in Science? Not so. It was a theosophical reason, Father."

Brett was very earnest, and very solemn. "It was my purpose, you understand, to reach the girl at the *exact moment* we had always seen her. We planned to make our Time before reaching her, coincident with hers of that given instant. Remember that. Consider then: At this other instant when now we were trying to see her through the myrdoscope, our Time-rate had carried us about 8,000 years into earth's future. But also, it had carried us some forty minutes into the girl's future.

"Not science now. Metaphysics, perhaps—and certainly Theology, and Theosophy. We were destined *to be with the girl during those forty minutes*. And we could not now look ahead and *see ourselves*—see our future actions.

"Father, you've spoken of that. What you said was true. It is not God's way that man should look at his own little future. Not best for us. The Almighty knows it, and has prohibited it. Chaos would result for we live upon hope. There was no scientific reason why the myrdoscope should not show us what we were destined to do during those forty minutes. Yet—it was dead. Dark, Inoperative.'

The girl screamed—a little voice, shrill with terror, an agony of sudden fear.

"And this now I know: With all the science in the world there are some things you can not do—those things which transgress the Creator's laws. Before them—against all scientific reason, logic—we must fail. You can not see your future; you can only live it once. Nor can you go back through Time to stop in your own Past; to live again your life—to do differently than you did before. It is unthinkable—impossible, even though now we have the scientific means to accomplish it. It is not the Almighty's plan—and He will not let us do it.

"We reasoned all this out. It was simple enough. We had our Time-switch which would change our Time-rate irrespective of the normal Time change inherent to our size.... That was what puzzled you awhile ago Frank? Well, now we used the Time-change mechanism.

"It brought us new sensations. Shock, a queer humming light pervading the vehicle, the air, our bodies. A lightness as though almost we were mere shadows of former selves. Specters, a ghost vehicle, humming with an infinite vibration.

"Presently that all wore away; or at least we grew used to it— so had there been anything in Space to see, as very soon there was, ourselves were the substance—all else were shadows.

"We went backward very slightly in Time. I suppose some forty minutes of the girl's Time. I tested it by the myrdoscope. The instrument flashed on! It was operating! A continuous *retrograde* action of the Time-mechanism was necessary to hold us upon that single given instant of the girl's existence. The calculation was intricate; I reached it, partly by mathematics, partly by experimentation with the myrdoscope. I saw fragments of the girl's immediate Past as our Time-change swung us into it. Saw her arrive alone in the woodland dell. Saw her lie down, at ease, with a security unsuspecting; saw the grinning, vicious little gnomes creep upon her; the leering giant appear. And made, then, another startling discovery—I'll tell you about it in a moment.

"At last I had the Time-change correctly gaged; we were—in relation to the girl—standing still in Time. Presently we again increased our size. An alteration of the Time-mechanism was needed; a progressive alteration. But this was simple to calculate and to adjust."

Frannie asked, "What was your discovery?"

He smiled. "Curious as always, little sister? It was that the giant was in the act of becoming *smaller!* The gnomes were growing in size!" He checked our chorus of exclamations.

"I will tell you now: This giant—these gnomes—were three beings who did not belong to the girl's world, they had come there from a greater world outside the atom. By means of science—such means possibly as we now were using with the vehicle—They had diminished their stature to the infinitely small. Had gone down and down into their tiny atom, to come upon the girl and her realm."

Again Brett waved us aside. "Not now, please! Oh, yes—I can tell you the structure of this, our little fragment of the material universe! But let me finish first about our voyage.

"With our Time-change corrected, the myrdoscope readily had picked up the image of the girl. A larger image, for we were 12,000 light-years closer to her. The same scene, stricken again of motion. The giant standing there; the gnome climbing upon the girl's ankle; and herself, just aware of her danger, with dawning terror on her face.

"The electro-telescope also was working now. Looking behind us, we could just see the last of the stars. And soon they were gone. A day of our conscious existence went by. At 3,000 light-years an hour we added 72,000 light-years of distance—a total from earth of about 84,000. The black abyss of Space had not remained empty. Off to one side had been a faint glow. A nebula; a patch of stardust. Through the telescope we could see stars—a complete starry universe. It was as large, no doubt, as that we had passed through.

"It gave us a new idea of the immensity of Space. Separated by some 30,000 light-years from our own universe of stars—of which the Solar System is so tiny a part—this other star-patch was equally as large. And yet it seemed to lie isolated in fathomless Space. It drifted by us and in a few hours was gone. And far off to the other side of us, another patch came past. And others; each several thousand light-years in extent; each isolated from all its fellows.

"We traveled another full day. Over 150,000 light-years from earth. Yet the girl's image was seemingly not coming nearer very rapidly. We felt the voyage would take too long, so again we increased our size."

I interrupted. "Had you calculated the girl's relative size?"

"Yes," he said. "In a moment, Frank, you shall have it. We—our vehicle—was 500,000 miles high, compared to earth. We increased it to 600,000. Our velocity also increased. At a million miles of height—I have made all my stated figures round numbers, but they are approximately correct—at this million-mile height, we reached normality to the girl. It simplified our mechanism adjustments. There was no longer a size-change necessary. A retrograde Time-change, equal to our own now normal rate of existence, held us at that same instant of her life.

"Our velocity was more than proportionately increased. To demonstrate that mathematically would be intricate—would involve several very complicated formulas, which would not interest you now.... We passed, distantly, a score or more of starry universes—to the sides, and above and below us—lying in every plane; and of every size and general extent, Some were small, a few thousand light-years like our own. Others immense; one which seemed 500,000 light-years at least in diameter.

"We reached ultimately a maximum velocity of about 90,000 light-years an hour. We had previously gone 150,000 light-years from earth. We traveled some eighty additional hours, not all at the maximum—for possibly half that time we were steadily accelerating. And at a total of 4,750,000 light-years from the earth, a faint glow of seeming phosphorescence showed in the blackness beneath us.

"There was a universe to one side, ahead of us. But this was a different light. A radiation from the Inner Surface itself. The Inner Surface of the hollow little atom within which all this Space and its infinitesimal whirling electrons is contained. They are immense suns, to us here on earth, but from the larger viewpoint they were mere electrons, whirling, flashing around in tiny orbits a thousand times a second.

"The girl and her realm, as we had thought, are on this Inner Surface of what we may choose to call an atom. Themselves—this girl and her people—are infinitesimal. This atom of ours is merely some tiny particle of matter in that other world from which the giant and the gnomes had descended. A tiny particle of matter. Call it a grain of sand, lying with trillions of its fellows upon some great ocean beach—lying there in the light of stars shining in infinite Space above it. Lying there for a single starlit night which is all eternity for us. A single starlit night—an eternity! Infinity, of Space and Time? Why, even now I have seen no more than an infinitesimal fragment of them!...

"The giant and gnomes were doubtless normally of the same size—only momentarily did they happen to be different.... Wait, Frannie, please! I can't tell it to you any faster.... The Inner Surface became visible to our telescopes at about 4,900,000 light-years. A realm of land and water. Vegetation. Strange of aspect, yet normal too, It stretched beneath us in every direction—a huge concave surface.

"We kept our size, but using the repellent force of this Inner Surface, I gradually cut down our velocity. Down more and more until that last light-year or so took us a week to traverse. The girl, Father, is approximately 5,000,000 light-years from here. We—our earth—maybe near the center of the void. I don't know. Perhaps we are much nearer the girl's side. It isn't important....

"The Inner Surface at last lay close beneath us. It took us an additional week of diminishing velocity to reach its atmosphere. I was cautious; I had the velocity under control always."

He paused a moment, seeming carefully to consider his next words. "I want you now to forget earth standards. Take the larger viewpoint exclusively. Let me speak of miles, not in relation to earth, but miles—in relation to the Inner Surface—which are 100 million times longer. Let me speak then of myself as again but six feet high; the vehicle, 52.8 feet high. Realize that by the larger standards I was but one-twentieth of a light-year from earth."

Dr. Gryce said gravely, "Your telescope would show a globe like the earth with very plainly at one-twentieth of a light-year of distance. You must explain, Brett, why you could not see it—or any of the great stars of our immediate universe."

Brett nodded. "We could not see the earth, because to our size it was merely a little orange. To be more exact, a ball about five inches in diameter. A tiny ball I could have hid in my hand, whirling out there in Space, spinning like a top on its axis to make your infinitesimal days and nights; traversing its entire orbit—a complete revolution around its little sun—more than three times every second!

"With these other standards, then, I want you to visualize us as we sat on the floor of the vehicle gazing down through the lower window. We were, say a hundred miles above the Inner Surface, just entering the upper strata of its atmosphere, and falling gently downward. Beneath us lay a broad vista of land and water; vegetation; forests; here and there patches of human habitation—houses, villages. It was a strange, unfamiliar landscape, yet not unduly abnormal. In every direction—as we dropped closer—it spread upward to our horizon. A rolling country; gently undulating hills, broad valleys—and off near the horizon a jagged mountain range. It seemed not far away; we could see black yawning holes in it; the mouths of caves, or tunnels, perhaps.

"The broad crescent lake lay directly beneath us. Trees bordered its banks; trees strange of shape—yet one would call them trees at once. A collection of low, flat-roofed buildings lay beside the water. A village—or a city. The buildings were queerly curved—seemingly crescent-shaped. They had no straight lines. They seemed generally of but one story, though a few were larger; and upon an eminence near the water stood one much larger; more ornate of shape than all the others.

"It was not a fantastic scene, but wholly rational to our own accepted standards. A sylvan atmosphere seemed to hang upon it. Trees and flowers were everywhere; the roof-tops seemed gardens as luxuriant as those beside the houses. The streets were broad and orderly; and beyond the city ribbons of roads wound out over the hills.

"A sylvan landscape, with an air of quiet peace upon it. I felt a sense of surprise. This was not modernity; nor a civilization more advanced than our own—nor yet was it barbarism. Later I knew it was decadence. A people who once had been far up the slope of civilization, over the peak, and now were coming down upon the other side. The peaceful, restful ease of decadence, which to complete the inevitable cycle of all human life ultimately would again bring them to barbarism.

"We saw these details as we fell gently toward the crescent lake. You will notice I have not mentioned color in the scheme, nor movement. Our Time-mechanism was operating. The scene beneath us was stricken motionless, since always we were holding to the same instant of its Time. An unreality lay upon it; a flat, shadowy grayness of aspect. An unnatural stillness. We dropped closer. A shadowy boat seemed on the lake—a boat with a sail. It lay there, immobile. The water was rippled by a breeze; but they were frozen ripples. And in the streets now we saw people and curious vehicles—all standing like waxen figures.

"The grove of trees—the woodland dell wherein the girl was

lying—was a short distance down the lake shore from the city. A single house was near it; but in the other direction was unbroken forest. An open space was there—a few hundred feet from the girl and her assailants. We decided to land there. We knew we were invisible as yet—a ghost of a vehicle, all in this same instant coming from Space to land upon the lake shore.

"We had not yet decided just what we would do. But it was necessary to land first. And necessary also for the vehicle to assume the Time-rate of this realm before we could leave it. When that was done we would be normal humans, to rescue the girl as best we might.

"We dropped into the little clearing at the edge of the lake, and gently came to rest—and upon the surface of the ground, since to us it would have had no substance; but within a foot of it, where, like a ghost hovering, I held us level. The unreality of us, I must repeat, was not to us apparent; we seemed solid—it was the ground, the forest about us which was unreal. Spectral trees; a gray twilight. I made sure that nothing was touching us. We were a few inches only above a soft-looking gray ground. We were ready to cut off our Time-change—to take our places normal to this new realm."

8

THE ENCOUNTER IN THE FOREST GLADE

Martt said, "I would have thrown off the Time-switch and rushed out at once. But Brett wanted to talk about it.

Brett smiled. "It was difficult for us to remember that no haste was needed. No haste—until we took the girl's Time-rate. And then we would need all haste possible. We discussed what we were to do. We had weapons—the electronic flash, for instance with which we could have struck down that giant as with a lightning bolt. But could we? I was not sure—not absolutely sure—that the weapon would be operative. Or that, perchance, this giant would not by some strange means be proof against it. A man sixty feet tall is no mean adversary. Suppose he held the girl before him? Would I dare attack?

"I suggested," Martt put in, "That we take the normal Time-rate of the girl, and be in hiding until the giant's size had dwindled to hers. The dwarfs were growing. But there would only be three of them, against two of us—and so far as we had seen they were not armed."

Brett went on. "That didn't seem a good plan. The giant's size was, we had calculated, rapidly dwindling. Within five minutes he would be the girl's size. But suppose, instead of standing there during those five minutes he picked up the girl—made off with her? It was too dangerous.

"At last we decided to make the vehicle, and thus ourselves somewhat larger. At the risk seriously of frightening the girl, we decided to take a stature larger than the giant. Thus, since he was not armed, we would have little difficulty keeping the girl from harm.

"The forest glade within which our vehicle was hovering was ample for the growth. We adjusted the mechanisms; and in a few moments of growth we had reached the determined point. We shut off the switches; the vehicle fell its few inches to the ground....

"The scene clarified. We were in a somber forest of dull, orange-colored vegetation. Above us was a deep purple sky, with a few drifting clouds, and stars gleaming up there in the darkness. They were the stars of that last universe we had passed; unnatural of aspect, for they seemed unduly close and unduly small.

"It was not day—nor yet was it night. A queerly shimmering twilight; shadowless, for the light seemed inherent to every-thing.

"We were aware of all this in an instant, but we did not stop to regard it, for Time now was passing. The girl and her assailants were now, we knew, in full motion. With the flash cylinders in hand we stepped hastily from the vehicle doorway.

"The forest trees were saplings no higher than ourselves. We plunged through them, came to the other glade. The girl was sitting up with hands pressed to her breast in terror—a tiny figure of a girl not as long as my hand. The dwarfs were so small I did not see them at first; they were standing beside her—an inch perhaps in height. The giant, with what drug acting upon him we could only guess, had dwindled until he was only about half our own present height. He had dropped his tree-bludgeon, which now was too large for him, and was stooping down to seize the girl. His leer, with the reality of motion upon it, was horrible.

"Momentarily we had stopped at the edge of the glade. The

figures there were aware of us. The girl screamed—a little voice, shrill with terror, an agony of sudden fear—at her assailants, and doubtless most of all at ourselves. The giant—I can no longer call him that since we saw him as no more than three feet tall—at our appearance he straightened. Stared at us. Surprise, then fear swept his ugly hairy face. He shouted something to his tiny companions.

"Martt's hand went up; he fired his cylinder. But he was confused—and the nearness of the girl to his mark made him aim high. The bolt missed; lodged harmlessly in a tree with a ripping of its bark. I rushed forward to seize our adversary, but he eluded me, leaped over the girl. I was afraid of trampling her—I stepped backward—clutched Martt, fearful of what he might do.

"It had all happened in a moment. The dwarfs had vanished; but the other man—he was now no higher than my knees—was standing by a tree behind the girl. He shouted again; and now the terror had left his face and he was grinning, I saw his hand go swiftly to his mouth. Had he taken more of his strange drug? Had he warned his two companions to do the same? I think so, for before my eyes he was swiftly diminishing in size. I knelt carefully beside the girl. Her figure—smaller than my foot and near it—was huddled into a little ball, her head against her upraised knees. She may have fainted; I did not heed her, save to be careful my movements did not strike her. With arm stretched over her I reached for the man. But he hopped away and eluded me. Still grinning. As small now as my little finger he stood half hiding behind a grass-blade. On hands and knees I pursued him. But like an insect, he was too quick for me. Smaller always until I was probing the grass with my fingers to find him—saw him momentarily like an ant in size as he leaped into a tangle of tiny grass-blades and was gone.

"I had forgotten my weapon. Illogically I had had no desire to kill that tiny figure—only to catch it. But Martt had had no such feelings. He was stomping around the glade—trying to stamp upon the other figures—and mumbling angrily to himself. I called to ask if he had caught them. He didn't know. He had seen them momentarily—seen them raise their hands to their mouths. But they had dwindled so fast, they were lost in a moment.

"The girl was unconscious, lying there in a huddled little heap. Gently I raised her, held her in the palm of my hand. She was white as a little waxen figure—white and beautiful; and so small I scarce dared to touch her with my huge rough fingers.

"Martt brought water from the lake. I rested my hand on the ground, with her still lying in it. And then presently she opened her eyes."

Brett paused, and as he gazed at each of us in turn I thought I had never seen his face so earnest. And there was upon it, too, a look almost of exaltation—a look which transfigured it. He added gently: "You three—my father, my sister, my friend, I have no need to hide from you my emotions. I think then—incongruously perhaps, for that little figure of girlhood lying there so soft and warm in the palm of my hand—I think then my love for her was born."

Hide his emotions! He could not had he wished. This love in his heart was written plain on his face, to soften it, to uplift it to something—or so it seemed to me—something just a little more than human. A touch, perchance, of divinity. And I think now that love does that—if only for some fleeting moment—to each one of us.

He went on very softly: "She opened her eyes. I was afraid she would be frightened. I tried to look very gentle, compassionate. I held my hand very still. I think that for an instant.

Martt and I stopped breathing…. She opened her eyes—met mine. I saw in hers a flash of terror. But something, strangely, must have conquered it—against all reason as she stared at me. Stared while the terror faded, and her little lips parted and smiled a welcome and a thanks…."

9

"DWINDLING GIANTS FROM LARGENESS UNFATHOMABLE"

There was not one of us who would have interrupted Brett when he paused to light an arrant-cylinder and to choose what next he would tell us. He was speaking softly, reminiscently, and with a curious gentleness

"I carried her to the vehicle showed it to her. Obviously she could understand nothing of my words; but she was very quick to read my gestures; smiling readily now, with her fear quite gone. And sitting up in the palm of my hand, with her arms flung about my thumb to steady her, she bade me raise her to my ear. Her words—the softest, the tiniest of human voices—what she said was wholly unintelligible, save that I understood her name was Leela.

"She stood beside a tree at a distance while we re-entered the vehicle and brought it down to a size normal to her; and came out of it to confront her."

Martt burst out: "I tell you that was when I realized how beautiful she is. Say, you never saw a girl like her—you can't describe it—"

"I'm not trying," said Brett with his gentle smile. "She met us—there by the vehicle—to us then, Frannie, she was about your size—perhaps a little smaller. She took our hands, laid them against her forehead as though with a gesture of welcome. And led us presently to her home—the house nearby. Her father (her mother is dead) her father is a musician. Noted—very high of rank and standing among his people. A kindly old man, with gray and black hair worn long to the base of his neck. We—Martt and I—didn't let ours grow, though as you see we took their mode of dress."

"How long were you there?" I asked.

"We slept perhaps three hundred times," he answered. "There are no days and nights—always that same half-luminous twilight. No change of seasons—or very little. It is nature in her softest mood. Nothing to struggle against—life made easy. Too easy… It was not we who learned Leela's language, but she, like an unnatural precocious child, who learned ours…. We created a commotion among the people; the ruler sent for us…. Oh, I have so much I'd like to tell you. But Martt can tell it—after—"

He checked himself suddenly. His words, some vague hint of what he almost had added, sent an ominous chill to my heart; and I saw, too, that Dr. Gryce had felt it, for a cloud came to his face and in his eyes I saw fear lurking.

But Brett went on at once: "I'd like to tell you of these people. A race at peace with nature and themselves. The struggle for existence all in the past. Decadence. The down-hill grade. Only by struggle can Man progress, Father. This race, with the peak of its civilization thousands of generations in its Past, gently resting, with the inevitable decadence drawing it inexorably back to the barbarism from whence it sprung. I'd like to tell you of their customs, their government—their mode of life…. Some other time—or Martt will tell you…. It was all so beautiful—so romantic… Music—their strange, beautiful arts—Music as Leela's father gave it—Art to take the place of Science and Industry…. You ask Martt to tell you about the dancing—the pageants, if you want to call them that, to which we went so many times with Leela…. But just now I'm tired—I think I've talked too much—and I'm worried—and it seems to press me, against all the logic of our Science, that I have no time to spend, telling all this to you...."

Brett, indeed, seemed suddenly tired, or perhaps harassed at the thoughts which had come to him. I had been so absorbed—as had all of us—that we had given no heed to the passing hours. Abruptly I realized that the room was chill with early morning; through the window I saw the flush of the eastern sky.

Martt followed my glance. "Why, its dawn! Brett's been talking all night."

Brett said strangely: "Too long! Father, this gentle race living out there in such seeming security had just been visited by beings from the great world outside it. A world known to them only by legend of their past ages which they scarce knew to be true or false. Those three assailants of Leela's—and other men like them—had suddenly appeared as dwindling giants coming down out of largeness unfathomable. They had already destroyed a city...."

Brett's voice had risen; he was talking faster now; and there was a touch of wildness in his tone—a wildness perhaps born of his exhaustion, and the emotional stress under which I knew now he had been laboring all night.

"Our arrival there, Father—the three assailants of Leela—I think the larger, him whom we have called the 'giant'—I think he is leader of the invaders from that greater world. Our appearance—our own power to change size which perhaps he observed there in the forest—must have frightened him. The invaders vanished. But at the end of those months we lived there—another of these giants was seen.

"They're coming back again—to threaten Leela and all her people! I came here to see you, Father—to tell you all I've told—and to leave Martt. But I'm going back—to do what I can against this threat—this invasion. And I want to go back to Leela. She—"

"She was afraid to come with us," Martt put in. "I wanted her to come—and now I want to go back with Brett. We've been arguing about it for days—he won't let me go back with him—he's stubborn—"

Brett reiterated: "I'm going back. I'm going alone. As soon as I've slept—I've got to sleep now—you, you'll excuse me— let me take a good long sleep—I'm too tired to argue about it now…. Good night, Frannie, dear—good night, Father—good night, Frank."

He was presently gone from the room. Dr. Gryce had been sitting beside me and I put my hand on his arm. His face was quite colorless; his voice, suddenly very old and helpless, was murmuring, "I don't want him to go out there again. I'm afraid—and I don't want him to do it…."

10

THE SOLITARY VOYAGER

"But Brett," I said, "there are one or two things I want to ask you. About your return voyage—for instance—"

It was mid-afternoon. Brett, thoroughly rested, was wholly himself again. Quiet, composed and smiling, but very determined; even a little grim. And I think he was a bit ashamed of the sudden, almost querulous way in which he had terminated his narrative and left us there in the observation room at dawn. He had had his sleep now; and had been alone for an hour with his father. Martt and Frannie had been called to them; I—an outsider—was not asked, or wanted. What took place there behind the closed door of the study, it was not for me to ask. But when they came out I knew that Brett had won. A questionable victory, for old Dr. Gryce was visibly broken; Frannie—pale and upon the verge of tears; and Martt for a time a trifle sullen; resentful that he was to be left behind. I think it hurt Brett—this fear he was bringing upon on those he loved. But he was very determined; convinced that it was the right thing for him to do.

"I start back tonight, Frank," he told me soberly as he emerged from the study.

"Oh," I said. "For how long will you be gone this time?"

He hesitated. A look, which even now my memory fails to interpret came to him. Then he smiled. "I don't know. But remember, Frank, I can return—with only those limitations the Almighty enforces—I can return to any point of earth-

Time I wish. As you will live it—well I shall aim to return here within a month."

It was then I asked him about the return voyage he and Martt had just made. "Brett, I've been wondering—did our aural ray guide you back?"

"Yes," he said. "On the voyage back, the first thing I did was to put the vehicle back through Time to a chosen instant at which I wished to arrive here on earth. When that was done, I held that instant always. We could not see the aural ray going out—when we looked back for it—for two reasons. One: Our Time had run far into earth's Future, and the ray was non-existent. The other: Even had we taken the proper Time-point, we were outrunning the light-rays themselves. In space, I mean, the aural ray left earth only with the speed of light. Our velocity exceeded that. You see? But on the return voyage we encountered the ray as we came in. A mere flash over the sky; but its characteristic color-bands guided us."

What he said about outrunning the light-rays made me think of the myrdoscope, the image of that girl—which they had received here on earth before the voyage—that image had crossed a space 5,000,000 light-years in extent. But when I mentioned it, he explained:

"The myrdal rays are not light, Frank but only akin to it. Their velocity—why, light beside them is a laggard. We have no way of computing the velocity of the myrdal rays But over a finite distance such as five million light-years—for practical purposes it is instantaneous....

"I wanted to tell you—I was confused last night—I meant to explain that coming back I used quite a different method from the outward trip, I chanced a disturbance of some of those outlying starry universes, and when we left the Inner Surface, I made the vehicle larger instead of smaller. The void of Space shrank until about us the universes were clustered like little patches of mist—many areas of glowing star-dust. I saw our own, with its spectrum of the aural ray, quite readily. And had readied it with a voyage of a few hours—and then reduced our size."

"And your Time," I said. "Brett, I didn't see the vehicle until it was almost entering the earth's atmosphere. And—just for an instant—it seemed not solid, but like a vague gray ghost Then suddenly it materialized."

He smiled and nodded. "Yes. That was when I took the earth's normal Time-rate."

The family joined us; we said no more. And that night Brett left us for his solitary voyage. I would not set down here in detail those last good-byes. Emotion repressed—it was what was not said that held a pathos I shall never forget. An outward attempt at lightness. Martt laughed, "Give my love to Leela." And Frannie said, "You tell her I'm jealous because she's so beautiful."

Just before Brett closed the door of the vehicle, Dr. Gryce spoke—the only thing he had said for an hour past.

"You'll be sure to come back, Brett? Within the month, lad?"

"Oh, yes. Yes, Father dear."

"Well—good-bye...."

Good-bye! I can think of no sadder word for human tongue to frame.

11

BRAVE LITTLE BEACON STRIVING
TO PIERCE INFINITY

That little month of anxious watching and waiting passed so
slowly! And yet so quickly, as one by one its golden moments
of hope drained away.

Brett did not return. A month, then a year, while Dr. Gryce
made me leave the Service, to enter his, that all my time might
be spent in watching.

A year; and now another year has passed. Brett would return
within the month. "With his Time-mechanism unimpaired, no
delay out there in the Beyond could have affected his return
to reach us during that first little month. With that passed and
gone, reason could only show the futility of expecting him ever.
Yet reason plays so small a part, when it would seek to kill hope.

The aural ray still burns—brave little beacon striving to
pierce infinity. Beside it, for those long, unreasoning hours
of vigil, Dr. Gryce sits and waits; silent, grayer and every day
visibly older. The possibilities of what could have happened
to Brett—that myriad of futile human conjectures—we have
long since ceased voicing. Alone I sometimes speculate. Has
Brett gone on into that outside world of which we all are only
a tiny atom? What is he doing? And then I tell myself, what is
it to me, save that it concerns Brett? The myriad, unfathomable happenings of Eternal Time in Infinite Space—what right
have I, one tiny mortal, to probe them?

The beacon burns to guide Brett back to us. Will he ever

come? I wonder. My brain, with its logic says he will not. But my heart says "Might he not come tonight?" Or with tonight passed, then tomorrow he will be here. Thus hope runs on and on, daunted but never broken. Blessed hope, to make possible a courageous living of this little life until we ourselves are plunged into that glowing Infinity of the Hereafter.

THE GIANT
WORLD

1

THE SUMMONS

I was startled. Yet I think that subconsciously I was prepared
for it; expecting it. The little cylinder flipped out of its tube and
dropped on my desk before me. My name was on it, glowing
with tiny luminous letters: *Frank Elgon, Interplanetary Mails,
Division 4, Great-New York.* It looked just like any other Depart-
mental message cylinder. But instinctively I knew it was not;
and my heart was beating fast as I clicked it open.

Relayed through Code Headquarters. I saw that on the small
rolled tape inside. And saw the signature, Dr. Gryce. It should
not have been startling, but my fingers were trembling as I
unrolled the tape and hooked it into the automatic decoder.
And I stood gripping my chair as the line of English letters
pricked themselves on the blank white sheet at which I was
staring:

Frank—I can not bear it any longer. We must go—we must
find Brett at any cost. Will you stand by us? Come at once.
Hurry.   DR. GRYCE

The GIANT WORLD

The giant grinned malevolently in the starlight.

My mind leaped back. I sat at my desk staring blankly, while in the office around me all the bustling activity of the accursed Interplanetary Mails faded before the surging visions of my memory. It was four years since that other momentous day when Dr. Gryce had sent for me. And I had gone to him; and listened amazed at his weird, fantastic theories. Our sun, planets, and stars—all the vastness of the star-filled heavens, he had told me then—were but the infinite smallness of a greater world. All this that we call our Celestial Universe was no more than an atom—of the giant world encompassing it.

Fantasy! Yet it had proved sober, tragic fact. Tragic, because Dr. Gryce's older son, Brett, had gone out there to that giant world. Gone, and never returned. Nor been heard from; four years now, while old Dr. Gryce at the end of his life waited despairingly.

I had known always that the time would come when Dr. Gryce would wait no longer. He would send for me—friend of Brett—and friend of his other two children, Martt and Francine. For a year every cylinder that had dropped on my desk had made my heart leap that it might contain this summons which now lay before me.

"I can not bear it any longer. Will you stand by us?" So simple an appeal! But I knew the turgid torrent of heartache—the final desperation of an old man's suffering—which prompted it.

Young Grante at the desk next to mine was sorting his pile of official communications newly arrived by the Venus mail. I turned to him.

"I'm going away," I told him. In spite of myself—an unfortunate mannerism when I am perturbed—my voice sounded gruff, ill-tempered. "There is no time to argue—will you please notify Official 4 that my—my post is vacant."

He raised his eyebrows. "Vacant?"

"Yes. I'm going away." I was on my feet. Outwardly calm, but within me was a seething emotion. Going away! Out there into the immensity of the Unknown, where my friend Brett had gone, not to return. Young Grante could not guess. He was thinking Great-London perhaps—or the Asiatic province. Or perchance, Venus, or Mars.

I laughed harshly. "Don't question me, Grante. Just tell them—my post is vacant."

I left the room with his amazed stare following me. In the corridor, through a window I caught a glimpse of the tenth pedestrian level; its crowd of people moving upon the diverse activities of their tiny lives. Already I felt apart from them.

Frank Elgon, Division 4. Presently, to such of them as knew me, I would be no more than a memory. "That young, rather quarrelsome Elgon, who walked out of his office in a temper, and vanished." They would say that, and then forget me.

I laughed again. But the thought brought a pang of regret, and a shudder.

In ten minutes I was within a pneumatic cylinder, speeding underground to the Southern Pennsylvania area, to the home of Dr. Gryce.

Martt and Frannie met me at the outer gateway. Their manner held a singular gravity. I had expected them to be excited, of course. But their grave, somber smiles of greeting, their instinctively hushed voices, seemed unnatural. This was no reckless, devil-may-care spirit of high adventure which I had anticipated the twins of Dr. Gryce would display. Sober drama. Their involuntary glances at the white house nestling against the hillside carried a foreboding.

Drama, but it seemed almost to be tragedy. My heart sank. There was something very wrong here with the Gryces; something more imminent than the fact of Brett's absence over four years.

But I said nothing. Dear little Frannie gave me her two hands. They were cold.

Martt said, "Thank you for coming, Frank. Father is—waiting for you." His voice, usually flaunting, mocking at everything with the reckless spirit of youth, chilled me with its queerly broken tone.

We crossed the flowering gardens to the white house standing so peaceful in the afternoon sunlight. Martt led the way. The twins were twenty-one years old now. Alike physically, and in temperament. Both smaller than average height; slim and delicate of mold; blue-eyed, and fair of hair. They were always laughing; carefree—the spirit of irresponsible youth. But not today. I regarded Martt, trudging ahead of me—debonair, jaunty of figure in his tight black silk trousers and loose white shirt, bare-headed, his crisp, curly hair tousled by the wind. But there was a slump to his shoulders, a heaviness to his tread. And little Frannie behind him: girlishly beautiful, with her tossing golden curls, her familiar house costume of gray blouse and widely flaring knee-length trousers. But there was upon her a preternatural solemnity; a maturity of aspect indefinable.

At the doorway Martt turned and fixed me with his somber, blue-eyed gaze. And spoke with the same queer hush to his voice.

"Father is upstairs, Frank. He is—dying. He wants very much to live until you arrive."

Upon the pillows in the darkened room lay Dr. Gryce's head with its shaggy, snow-white hair, the mound of the sheet betraying his pitifully wasted body.

Martt said softly, very gently, "Frank is here, Father. You see he came in time—plenty of time."

But the head, with face to the wall, did not move; no stirring marked the fragile body lying there.

Martt gave a cry; with Frannie he rushed to the bedside. It was all too evident. In a moment Martt stood up, leaned silently against the bedpost, a hand before his eyes as though dazed. And Frannie knelt at the bed and sobbed.

We expect death all our lives, yet the instinct of life within us never ceases to feel a shock, and a revulsion. For a long time these children of Dr. Gryce did not move or speak. Then Frannie leaped to her feet. Her face was tear-stained; but her sobs were suddenly checked, and her eyes were blazing.

"Martt! His last wish—the very last thing he said—was that we go out ourselves and find Brett, He said it—he said Brett might need us—his dying wish. And I'm going, and so are you. We've got to, Martt! And we want Frank with us. Oh, Frank, you'll go with us, won't you? Out there—to join Brett?"

The burial was passed. We had not spoken of our enterprise, but it had never left my thoughts. This boy and girl so newly come to maturity—but I was twenty-nine. Upon me would fall the main responsibility.

We sat at last in Dr. Gryce's study—the three of us alone—to discuss our task. With the first poignancy of their shock and sorrow already dulled by time, upon the faces of Martt and Frannie was stamped grimly their simple purpose.

"But, Martt," I said, "Brett's vehicle was very intricate. It traveled in Space—but in Time as well. And grew gigantic in size. Your father's genius built it. But we have no such genius to build another—"

"You forget," he interrupted. "Think back, Frank. That day you came here. And we showed you the models of the vehicle. There were four of them—"

Then I remembered. Dr. Gryce had shown me four small models. One he had sent back into Time. A flash, like a dissipating puff of vapor it was gone into the Past; still here in Space above the taboret on which it was standing, but vanished with centuries of Time to hide it from my sight.

Another of the models, with Time unchanged, Dr. Gryce had sent into Infinite Smallness. I remembered watching it dwindling; a speck, a pinhead, then invisible even to the microscope.

Two of the models were left. Martt and Frannie, but seventeen years old then, had taken one into the garden. Had started it growing in size. I recalled our frantic efforts to check its growth, lest it demolish the house. This was the one in which Martt and Brett had gone to the giant world and in which Brett had returned alone to that distant part of our universe.

One model had remained. I had never thought of it since. Martt was saying, "…and we still have that last model. Father kept it very carefully." Martt's smile was wistful with the memory. "I think he—Father—had a premonition that he would not live to carry out his purpose…. The model is here."

He opened a locked steel box. Again I gazed silently at that small cube of milk-white metal—a cube the length of my forearm, with its tiny tower on top, its glasslike balcony, its windows and its doors.

"It's all complete," said Martt. "And I know how to operate it."

Frannie said with a touch of breathlessness, "For a month past, Father has been gathering the necessary instruments. And the supplies—you see he—he really thought he was going to live—"

"We're all ready," Martt added "We will increase this model to normal size. Load it with our supplies, We can start tomorrow, Frank."

Five million light-years from Earth! Who of finite human mind can conceive such unfathomable distance! Yet, as I crouched on the floor of the vehicle gazing down at the radiance emerging from the black void which was our first sight of the Inner Surface, the distance had seemed no more than gigantic. We were, in size, many million times our Earthly stature. The tiny Earth, from our larger viewpoint, was a little orange spinning above us in the void—a mere one-twentieth light-year away.

Martt, for all his youth, had proved competent. He had made the trip once before with Brett; he handled the vehicle carefully, and with skill. He said now, as we three crouched by the floor window, "We'll soon be down to the atmosphere, Frank. I'm checking our fall—we want no errors—"

We were reversed in Time—holding very nearly at a single instant, so that on the Inner Surface the time now was the same as it had been when we left the Earth.

We argued the point; Martt said, "I think when we land—we should choose the point in Time about four years beyond Brett's landing. So that it will be four years to us—and also to him. Don't you?"

"We decided upon that, so that we would reach the Inner Surface and find Brett had been there four years. It seemed to strike a greater normality. Find Brett! Would we find him? I wondered, as I knew Martt and Frannie were wondering. But in our plans we always took it for granted.

The radiance beneath us grew brighter. And at last we entered the upper strata of atmosphere, falling gently downward. It was a fair, beautiful land, as Brett and Martt had said. A sylvan landscape, with an air of quiet peace upon it. A broad vista of land and water; patches of human habitation—houses, villages; a city.

Martt was at the telescope. "Pretty good, Frank! I've hit it—I see the city—off there, isn't it? And the crescent lake."

He changed our direction slightly. As we dropped, the broad crescent lake lay beneath us. Trees bordered its banks; and to the right was the city of low-roofed, crescent-shaped buildings banked with flowers. And beyond the city a rolling country of gently undulating hills, with a jagged mountain range up near the horizon.

From this height it was a visibly concave surface. And it was gray and colorless, for we were passing abnormally through its Time. Then Martt threw off the Time-switch; we took the normal Time-rate of the realm. And in size we were also normal.

At a height of perhaps a thousand feet Martt held us poised above the city. "They'll see us now," he said. "If—if Brett is down there he'll recognize us. I'll land in the grove where we landed before. We'll give Brett time to get there to meet us."

With the Time-switch off, color and movement had sprung into the scene. The forests were a somber growth of dull, orange-colored vegetation. The water was a shimmering purple; and above us was a purple sky, with faint clouds, and dim stars up there—stars which seemed very small and very close.

The white houses gleamed and glowed in the starlight. Yet it seemed not night; nor day either. A queerly shimmering twilight. Shadowless, as though everything were vaguely phosphorescent.

In the broad city streets there was movement. Vehicles; people. And the people now were gathered in groups, staring up at us.

We landed in the little clearing at the edge of the lake near the city. And now at the last, Frannie gave voice to the fear which was within us all. "Oh Frank, do you think Brett will be here?"

There were human figures in the nearby thickets. I saw them through the windows, but we were too busy with the landing to look closely. The vehicle came to rest. Martt and I flung open the door. The vegetation was thick near by; we stepped from the vehicle onto a soft, mossy sward, and stood in a timid group, with tumultuously beating hearts.

"Martt! Frannie! Frank!" It was his voice! Brett was here! And we saw him step from a thicket. His familiar voice; his familiar figure, but so fantastically garbed that it brought to me a wild desire to laugh, for I was half hysterical with the relief of seeing him.

Frannie cried, "Brett! My brother! You're all right, Brett, aren't you? I'm glad you're all right."

Under stress, how inarticulate are we humans! I said awkwardly, "How are you, Brett? We thought we'd come and see you."

He took Frannie in his arms. And wrung Martt's hand, and mine, while his strange companions stood in the background among the trees watching us.

"Of course I'm all right," he declared. "And terrifically happy." A shadow crossed his face; his glance went to the vehicle's doorway. "Father didn't come with you?"

Then Martt showed a wisdom far beyond his years. This was no time to bring sorrow to Brett. Martt said smoothly. "Father is better than he has ever been, Brett. We'll tell you—later."

"Good! That's fine!" Brett's face was radiant. "You're just in time, you three. I'm to be married tonight."

But even then as I wrung his hand again, and congratulated him, I had a premonition that it was not to be.

2

STOLEN INTO SMALLNESS

"Life is pleasant here," said Brett, "Pleasant, and indolent. It does not make for progress, but it is happiness—and I'm beginning to wonder if that is not best, after all."

We were sitting in an arcaded passage on the roof of the home where Brett lived. Crescent archways opened to the roof, where stood banks of vivid flowers, with a vista of the city beyond. The building seemed of baked earth, rough like adobe, and of dull orange color. It was a two-storied, crescent-shaped structure, set upon a wide street-corner near the edge of the city. The home of Leela's father. I had never forgotten Leela—the girl Brett and Martt had rescued from the giant on their first visit here. Brett had fallen in love with her. It was she whom tonight he was to marry. And this was her father's home—Greedo, the old musician.

"I have lived here with them six months," Brett said.

Martt exclaimed, "Six months! "Why Brett, you have been gone four years!"

We had miscalculated the Time-change of the vehicle. Our purpose had been to strike this realm of the Inner Surface at a point in Time which to Brett would be four years. But now we found it six months only.

Brett smiled. "I'm glad you didn't postpone your arrival. You've no idea how pleased I am to have you—tonight of all nights."

We had not yet seen Leela, or her father. Brett said that Leela would be up presently to greet us. The city was excited over our coming. A crowd was gathered in the street before the house; Brett had made them a brief speech; Frannie, Martt and I had stood at the parapet and waved to them.

Then Brett had spoken of a younger sister of Leela's. Her name was Zelea—they called her Zee.

Martt sat up at this. "Where was she when we were here before?"

"Away," said Brett. "She was too young to meet a man then. Only now has she come to be sixteen. You'll like her, Martt. I want you to like her."

"I will," said Martt enthusiastically, "if she's anything like Leela."

"You were telling us about the life here." I suggested. "We always called this land the Inner Surface—"

"Yes," he agreed. "It is concave, like the inner shell of some great, hollow globe. Within the space it encloses—" He gestured to where, through the arcade, a segment of purple, star-filled sky was visible. "All that which we of Earth called the Celestial Universe is enclosed by this concave shell. You would think that this must be a gigantic region—" He smiled again. "It is not. Compared to our present enormous size, I imagine the circumference of this Inner Surface is not unduly great. I don't know. These people have not explored very far. They are not wanderers—they are too indolent, too contented, to wander."

He paused to drink from a shallow receptacle which stood before us, and offered Martt and me what appeared to be arrant cylinders to smoke.

"I have learned a little of the language. Proper names are impossible to translate. But the meaning of their word for this land, I call in English, Romantica. The romantic land. It is, I fancy, about five hundred miles square. Beyond it lie forests and mountains. No one here has ever penetrated them. There are wild beasts, birds, insect life—and fish and reptiles in the water. But they are not dangerous—not aggressive. It is not because of them that these people avoid exploration. It is— just indolence."

"I don't wonder," I said. "This is very peaceful here—I have no desire to do anything in particular." From the city streets a drone of activity floated up to us; but it was almost somnolent.

"It's always like this," said Brett. "Almost no change of seasons—the light always the same. There is no disease here— or very little. Food—grains, and what we would call vegetables, grow abundantly in this rich soil. The trees give milk—even the bark and pulp of them are edible. Life is easy. There is nothing to struggle against.

"Through generations it has made the people kindly. There is little crime. No struggle for land, or food or clothing. Crimes involving sex—" He gestured. "Wherever humans exist there will be crimes of that origin. But our women here are very sensible, and when a woman does what is right—well, you know, don't you, that most deeds of violence into which men plunge over women have a woman's wrong actions at the bottom of them? There is little of that here, for the women take care that there shall not be.

"So they call their country Romantica. They are not a scientific people. They do not struggle for advancement. Art has taken the place of science. Painting. Sculpture. Music. They have developed music very far. It has a soul here. It speaks—it sings—it seems a living entity. It is—what music ought to be but seldom is—the pure voice of love, of romance.... I was telling you about our country. Most of its population live in villages, and in individual dwellings strewn about the hills. There are but two large cities. This one—the largest—they call Crescent. Or at least their word for it suggests the shape of the lake. The other city is about fifty miles from here"—he gestured again—"off there where you see the line of mountains. They call it Reaf. It's a quaint city. Built largely over the water—rivers there—hot, subterranean rivers which rush underground—under the mountains. They go—who knows where? No one has ever been down them. The mountains are honeycombed with caves, tunnels, passages leading within, and up. Always up. But into them no one has ever penetrated. Legends tell fabulous tales of a great world up there. The giants, we think—"

When Brett and Martt had first come here, giants had appeared. Dwindling giants—strange, savage beings of half-human aspect. They had appeared—no one knew from where. Growing smaller until they were normal size to this realm. Not many had been seen. Some had kept on dwindling; they had grown so small, when attacked, that they had become invisible. At the thought, I moved my foot involuntarily with a shudder of uneasiness. Here on the floor beside me now, men like beasts might be lurking, so small I could not see them. Yet in a moment they might grow to a stature greater than my own....

Men like beasts!... And I remembered that, with size gigantic, they had destroyed the third city of Romantica.

Upon Brett's face lay a cloud of apprehension. "We have never heard from them since. It is thought—I think myself—that they came from the subterranean rivers, or through the underground passages of the mountains. I conceive this concave surface upon which we're living to be the inner surface of a shell. It may not be very thick there at Reaf. Above it—beyond it—up or down are mere comparative terms—beyond it must lie some vastly greater outside world. This whole realm is doubtless within an atom of that greater world. It would be a convex surface up there—with a sky and stars beyond....

"We have never seen the giants since that time when Martt and I rescued Leela. Everyone here seems to have forgotten them—" Brett's voice was heavy with apprehension. "These people are so trustful! They forget so quickly! No one worries. Our rulers here—a venerable man and woman long past the age when death is expected—are so gentle, kindly, that they can not imagine harm coming to their people. They have forgotten the Hill City which the giants destroyed. Trampled upon it! Six or eight giants—they must have been several hundred feet tall—stamping, kicking the buildings! I've been there—I've seen the ruins—strewn for miles—and with buildings, colonnades and terraces mashed into the ground! There were no more than half a thousand people surviving that destruction of the Hill City—and thousands died. But everyone says now, 'The giants are gone. We are safe.' "

Brett's voice had risen to a swift vehemence. "It's been like living on a volcano to me, all these months. There are no weapons here. My own few flash-cylinders—of what use would a tiny flash of lightning be against beings so gigantic! We've got to do something. For if those giants come again—"

A step sounded in the oval doorway near at hand. Leela stood smilingly, deprecatingly before us.

Brett said, "Come here, Leela. This is my sister, and my friend, Frank Elgon, And here's Martt."

Leela advanced hesitantly, her face a wave of color as she met our gazes. She was smaller, and even slighter than Frannie, her figure adorned and revealed by its single, simple garment—more like a short, glistening veil than a dress. Her hair was long and dark, caught by a band at her neck, and flowing free beneath. Her arms and legs were bare. At her wrists, gray-blue bands with small tassels; on her feet, queerly high-heeled wooden sandals, with tasseled thongs crossing on her ankles. The sandals clacked as she walked; her step was mincing, with a suggestion of the Orientals of our Earth.

Brett eyed the sandals with a humorous twinkle. "For why are those, Leela?"

Her blush heightened. "In honor of our guests. I thought you would like them."

With a swift gesture, she stooped, untied the thongs and cast the sandals off. Her feet were very white, small and delicately formed, with rounded, polished nails stained pink. She stood untrammeled, lithe and graceful as a faun.

"I am glad to meet Brett's sister—and his friend. And you, Martt—I am glad to see you again." Her voice was soft as a Latin's. She shook hands with Martt and with me, and returned Frannie's affectionate embrace.

As I saw them together—these two girls of different worlds—I was struck with the dissimilarity of them, Pert, viva-cious little Frannie, blue-eyed, fair of hair—brown-skinned from the outdoor life she loved. And Leela—smooth, white skin, dark hair and luminous eyes, a fragile grace to her every moment. None of my words are adequate. There was about her an aura of romance; a strange wild spirit of something for which, every man in his soul has a longing; a beauty with a quality—ethereal—half human, but half divine.

A twinge of conscience came to me that I—Frank Elgon—could think such thoughts and see such beauty in any girl who was not Frannie.

Leela was saying, "My father would have you come down soon. And Zee is down there—Zee is very much excited, Brett. There is so much to do before tonight—"

Brett's arm was around her. "And you—of course you're not excited, are you, Leela?"

She returned his caress, embarrassed further by his teasing. He added, "We will be down presently."

"Yes," she said; and with a pretty gesture, she left us.

The sandals lay discarded on the floor. Brett gathered them up; regarding them tenderly. "She is so easy to tease, I love to do it. But if you try that with Zee—"

"You shouldn't tease her," said Frannie. "She's a darling. I love her already."

Brett's wedding day! For all his quiet, whimsical teasing of Leela, the love he bore her enveloped him like a shining cloak. Yet his father, whom he loved so dearly, was dead, and Brett did not know it. I whispered to Martt about it later.

"I think we should not tell him," said Martt. "Not until we have to."

And we did not. Looking back on it now, how much was to happen to Brett—to Martt, to us all! What fearsome things— danger, desperation, despair—were to be our allotted portion before we even thought again of old Dr. Gryce who was dead!

Brett was to be married that evening—a public festival and ceremony over which the whole city was in an anticipatory fever.

"The festival of lights and music," said Brett. "They hold it at periodic times. It is a wonderful sight. It generally includes a marriage—girls find it romantic. Leela selected it for us. Greedo is in charge of it—Leela and Zee always take part in its music. We must go down—they are waiting for us—there is so much for them to do between now and this evening."

"I'll help," said Frannie. "Come on, Martt—I guess you want to meet Zee, don't you?"

We found Leela's father to be a grave, black-robed, kind-faced old man of an age indeterminate. Sixty, or eighty, I could not have told. In vigorous health, evidently. His figure was spare, straight, but not tall. His thick, gray-black hair he wore long to the base of the neck.

He greeted us quietly, with an admirable dignity commanding immediate respect.

"You are a musician," I said, after we had been talking for a time. "Brett has told us something about your music here. It must be very beautiful."

He smiled. "Music is a wonderful thing. It ennobles. There is in it a touch of something beyond our poor human understanding. A touch of what you call Divinity."

"You speak our language very well," I exclaimed.

"A language is not difficult. All minds are similar—that is why music can make so universal an appeal." His voice was earnest, his eyes sparkling. It was the subject most absorbing to him.

I said, "You teach music—"

He raised a deprecating hand. "Yes. But that is nothing, I teach the fundamentals"—he struck his breast—"the rest comes from within. For myself, I am a mere retailer of sound. A peddler of something someone else has made. The composer—he is the real artist. I have hoped that some day Leela will compose. Brett has promised that he will urge her…. Just now, she sings." He twinkled at Leela. "I fear she thinks she sings very well. Pouf! It is nothing! She, too, is only a sound-peddler."

With a burst, Zee entered the room. A smaller replica of Leela. Yet how different! She came like a mountain torrent tumbling from the hillside. Her short, dull-red draperies whirled about her elfin figure. Her dark eyes were blazing. Black hair, flying over her shoulders with her tumultuous entrance.

"Father! That is not so!" She stamped one of her bare feet,

then rose on strong, supple toes and whirled half around. The muscles stood out beneath the smooth satin skin of her calves. "Leela, why do you let him say such a thing? You sing beautifully." She whirled back. "And what am I, then?"

The old man was wholly unperturbed. "You, Zee? Why, you are a peddler of movement. Very swift, tempestuous movement, generally." He added to me, "She thinks she is an artist. She is not. She is only a dancer."

It was what on Earth would have been termed late evening when we started for the festival. Greedo, with his two daughters, had left half an hour before.

We were dressed now in the fashion the country. Brett had suggested it; Martt had insisted upon it. I remembered with what a jaunty swagger Martt had worn his clothes upon his return to Earth that other time. He was dressed similarly now. A cloth shirt of glaring green, with a high, rolling collar in front, and low in the back; short trousers very wide and flapping at the knee. The trousers were a lighter green, with dark green stripes; his stockings were tan; and his green shoes were long and pointed. Over his shirt was a short tan jacket, wide-shouldered and with puffed sleeves, and bangles dangling from elbows and wrists. And there was a skirt to the jacket, rolling upward at the waist.

My own costume was in the same fashion; and though it was a sober gray, befitting my more mature years, I felt for a time awkward and foolish in it. But when in the crowded city streets I found that no one seemed particularly to remark me, I soon forgot it.

Brett wore a long cloak; I did not see how he was dressed. Frannie also wore a cloak. Just before leaving she tossed it aside, and stood before me, waiting for my admiration, with her characteristic twinkle, and her pert upflung face daring me to disapprove. Even by contrast with Leela and Zee, to my eyes at least Frannie was very pretty. She wore the single draped garment with silver cords crossed at her breasts to shape her figure; and with banded wrists, and tasseled bands above the knees. Her blond curls were tied with flowing tassels. The whole costume, a gray and blue, with a single deep-blue flower in her hair. And thin, flexible sandals on her little feet.

She eyed me. "Do you like me, Frank?"

"I—why, why—Frannie—" I would have told her then that I loved her, as I had very nearly told her myriad times in ten years past. But who was I to ask the love of any girl? A sorter of planetary messages, poor as a towerman in the lower traffic! "I—why yes, Frannie. Of course I like you. You're—beautiful."

She had a quaint little circular hat, stiff and round, with a dull-red plume and a tassel. We men wore hats of a solidly wooden aspect—low, round crowns and triangular brims. Martt's was sea-green, with tassels all around its brim. But mine and Brett's were sober gray, and unadorned.

We started on foot. The city streets were dim in the luminous twilight. Overhead, the sky with its thin-strewn stars was cloudless. A holiday aspect was everywhere. Crowds of people were in the streets. Young men and girls, gay with laughter. Most of them were cloaked. A vehicle, with runners like a sleigh gliding over the grassy pavement, drawn by a squat, four-legged animal, went by us. It was jammed with girls; one of them leaned out and waved at me. Her slim white arm came down; her hand twitched off my hat, sent it spinning. I caught a glimpse of her face; dark, laughing eyes, a mouth with mocking lips stained red....

The sleigh passed on.

With Brett leading us we turned toward the lake. Most of

the crowd seemed to be heading that way. Occasionally we were recognized. Stares of interest at us, the strangers, and cheers for Brett.

He said to me, "They're all very happy, Frank. Like children." I fancied that he sighed—he, for whom this night of all nights should have been his happiest.

In a group, with the swirling merrymakers about us, we made our way to the lake shore. The water was rippled by a gentle night breeze; the stars gleamed on the water surface with tiny silver paths. Boats were here—double canoes with outriders; and a few sailboats, small, single-masted, with triangular and crescent sails.

We found a small canoe; Brett sculled it with a broad-bladed paddle. Other boats were around us. A long canoe with a dozen sweeping paddles shot by us with the racing strokes of its men, and with shouts from its laughing girls. Another, smaller, turned over. Its men swam, and righted it. They climbed aboard, hauling up the girls. The wet draperies clung to them; they came up like dripping, gleeful water-sprites, tossing their black hair…. A barge went slowly along, drawn by two canoes. A lighted canopy was over its occupants—a huge, woven garland of flowers. The canopy gleamed with spots of vivid-colored lights.

"The luminous flowers," said Brett. And I saw that the large purple blossoms were gleaming with a purple light—a phosphorescence inherent in them; and red blossoms, like crimson lanterns; and others orange, and green. Music floated upward from the barge, soft and sweet over the water. The tinkle of strings—the voices of girls singing, and men humming with a deeper background of harmony….

A night for love-making. The night romantic. Brett's wedding night—and yet, he had sighed. I knew why, for upon my own heart lay a weight of apprehension, heavier because it was so incongruous. Martt quite evidently did not feel it—he was shouting and laughing constantly with his pleasure. A girl from a neighboring boat tossed him a large, blood-red, glowing blossom. It fell short, went into the water and slowly sank, staining the water with its red light. Martt all but turned us over trying to rescue it.

Frannie, too, seemed gay. I tried to smile; but I felt that it was forced. The depression upon me would not be shaken off. It grew to seem almost sinister. The very atmosphere of happiness around me seemed to intensify it. These merry-makers—in the midst of life.... At such a moment as this, death could choose to strike....

"Look!" shouted Martt. "The lights off there—is that where we're going?"

A patch of gay-colored lights gleamed from over the water ahead. "Yes," said Brett. "An island there, where they hold the festival. It's not far."

It was an irregular circular island, a mile perhaps in extent. The lake waters indented it with a hundred tiny bays, inlets, and narrow, placid waterways. We ascended one of them. The surface of the island was gently undulating, and wooded, with mossy dells—nooks arched with the luminous flowers. Nooks for lovemaking.

The whole island was strewn thick with the flowers; they grew upon tall, single stems—gay-colored lanterns nodding in the breeze. Beneath them were laughing couples; some hidden, sought and found by groups of marauding girls, to seize the man and laughingly whisk him away. And everywhere was music, soft as an echo....

We ascended the narrow waterways, came to a lagoon with a glassy surface wherein a thousand spots of the lantern-flowers were mirrored like colored stars. Near the shore here, beyond a dock at which we landed, was a broad enclosed space with an arcade of the lantern-flowers arching over it. Brilliant with their light. Most of the crowd seemed congregated there—a milling throng on the level floor inside, with liquid strains of music mingling with the shouts and laughter.

"We'll go in there," said Brett. "I'll find seats for you—then I must leave, to join Leela and her father. There is to be a musical program. But first—just Greedo, Zee and Leela, and our marriage. Most of the music comes afterward."

Within the arcade the lights blended into a kaleidoscope of color. All the cloaks were discarded now. Costumes vividly splashed as a painter's palette. Heavy perfumes. And that soft, echoing music. I could not tell its source.

At one end of the room was a raised, canopied platform, with doors behind it. Most of the crowd were choosing low seats, like stools ranged in rows. Brett got us settled.

"I'll leave you now—and meet you over there by the right-hand end of the platform, afterward."

He left us. With Frannie between us, Martt and I sat quiet, watching and listening. We had not long to wait. The light around us began to dim; sliding curtains were obscuring the flowers over us. A hush fell upon the crowd. The soft music was stilled. A hush of expectancy.

The arcade was in gloom. The light on the platform intensified. A deep-red glow, with a single spot focused upon a small, raised dais. Into the red glow came Greedo, robed unobtrusively in black. He was carrying a crescent frame of strings. He seated himself, and in the silence swept his hands across the strings. His fingers plucked them like a harp; and then his other hand slid upon them. The staccato notes rippled clear as a mountain rill, soft, muted to seem an echo of music. And blended with them was a low, crying melody—a fragment, then silence.

Leela had appeared. She crossed through the red glow, mounted the dais, and stood in the silver light—Leela, robed to her feet in a misty silver veil through which her figure vaguely was outlined. She stood there drooping—a Naiad veiled in the fountain mist.... Then Greedo's music sounded. And Leela sang.

It was like nothing I had ever heard before. Music, toned strangely, with strange intervals to make it neither major nor minor. Not happiness, nor yet sadness. A wistfulness. A longing. But with the promise of fulfillment.

I listened, breathlessly; and the arcade around me faded. Greedo's figure in the shadow was forgotten. There was only the white figure of Leela; her face, the purity of girlhood, her eyes half closed, her lips parted with the song. Nothing else—save myself. I stood in a void, stretching out my arms to Romance. All that I had ever dreamed, and vaguely longed for without understanding what it meant, was upon me. All that woman could mean to man—the spirit of the ideal never to be attained in mortal flesh—seemed suddenly attained. Romance—that thing elusive—intangible as a thought in the vaguest of dreams. It was mine!

The song ended. Applause rang out. Leela was gone.

Martt breathed beside me, "Frank! Wasn't that—wonderful! It was like—Look, here comes Zee!"

Zee was on the platform—a whirlwind of veils, stained by the red light, white limbs flashing as she whirled. Greedo's music was faster now. Snapping staccato, with a thrum of melody. The lights changed to a mingled riot of color within which Zee was dancing. An elf. A sprite of the woodland, with tossing hair and fluttering arms; and a laughing face.... A figure in the fairy-tale of a child....

But only for a moment. Then the dance slowed. Maturity came suddenly. Zee mounted the dais, and the light there was abruptly green. She stood in an attitude of terror, her eyes wide, hands before her, posturing with horror.

It made my heart leap. For an instant I fancied it had been real. But the light turned silver. The horror faded into a passion of love, her white arms extended, her breasts rising and falling beneath the veils, her red lips parted with passionate longing. The abandonment of youth—so young, with newly awakened passion as yet but half understood. Then again she was whirling around the platform, leaping on her bare toes, light as a faun....

Behind me, suddenly a woman screamed! The reality of a long scream of terror! Greedo's music ceased. The lights wavered. Zee was gone. A scream from the audience; then another. A chaos of mingled cries. Clattering of feet. Stools overturned.... Someone fell against me. I went down, recovered and climbed upright. The audience was in a panic. I heard Martt shout, "Look, Frank! Look there over the water!"

People were pushing me—surging to escape from the arcade. Shouting. Calling to one another. And the woman behind me was still screaming.

I saw it then. Through the open side of the arcade, out a mile or more over the water, the great giant figure of a man was standing, waist-deep in the lake, his naked torso towering a hundred feet above it. A giant, wading in the lake, his face grotesque, malevolently grinning in the starlight!

The crowd within the arcade was in a wild panic of terror. I was pushed and shoved, knocked down by heedless, rushing figures. Everyone was trying to get outside. In a moment I was swept away. I could not get back to where I was sitting, or even tell where the spot had been. Martt and Frannie I could not see; the place was all a dim chaos of disheveled, panic-stricken figures. A moment before they had been so gay and jaunty!...

A girl rushed past me. The veiling had been torn from her shoulders. Her eyes for an instant met mine, as she searched my face hoping to recognize in me the companion from whom she had been separated. Her dark eyes were wide, red-rimmed with fear. Her face, with all the beauty of youth gone from it, was chalk-white.

She turned and rushed away from me. I thought again, "In the midst of life... why, this is horrible!" That giant off there—he could wade to the island in a few moments....

I fought my way out of the arcade, out under the trees by the edge of the lagoon. There was more room out there. In the starlight I could see figures rushing aimlessly away, scattering under the lantern-flowers... others hurriedly crowding the boats. One boat was overturned. I wondered vaguely if the struggling figures in the water would be drowned.

Back near the wall of the arcade I saw a girl's figure running. It seemed familiar. Was it Fannie? I dashed after her. But people running in between us blocked me. I lost sight of her; saw her momentarily as she seemed to dart around the farther arcade corner. But when I got there, she was not in sight. Was it Frannie? Had she gone this way? Or into that door, back into the rear of the arcade?

I stood in doubt. Then I saw Brett, running past me, out under the lantern-flowers some fifty feet away. His cloak was discarded; he was bareheaded. Brett in his marriage robe! Black and white, with golden tassels gaily dangling from the

rolled skirt of his jacket. He was disheveled; as he ran, I saw
him tear off the jacket impatiently and toss it away.

"Brett! Oh, Brett!"

He stopped; whirled toward me. "Frank! Where's Frannie—
and Martt?"

"I do not know," I said. "I lost them. That giant—"

"The giant is wading the other way now." He pulled me past a
thicket, and pointed. I could see the back of the giant's naked
shoulders, towering up against the stars. He was going the
other way—wading toward the far-distant opposite lake shore.
And now against the island's banks, the waves the giant made
were beginning to pound.

Brett said: "I don't know where Leela is. I was in there with
her—and with Zee. I rushed out when the alarm came—when
I went back they were gone." He stood irresolute. "We must
find them, Frank. And get back home." He drew a long breath.
"It has come, you see, as I feared."

"I thought I saw Frannie," I said. "Running—that way. But
I'm not sure. I lost sight of her—"

From behind the pavilion came a scream. The scream of a
girl. Familiar…. The blood drained from Brett's face. "Leela!"

And then I heard Frannie screaming from there also. We ran.
The two girls were standing there clinging to each other. They
seemed unharmed. But they were trembling, shuddering, arms
gripping one another.

"Leela! What is it?" Brett held her off, regarding her. "You're
not hurt, are you? What is it?"

We four seemed alone here beside the arcade. Lantern-flowers were over us; a thicket was near by. Frannie's arms were
around me.

"Frank—oh—" She choked; she seemed struggling to tell me
something.

I held her close. "You're not hurt, Frannie. Just frightened. What became of Martt?"

Oh, horrible! What gruesome, horrible thing was this! Within my arms I could feel her sensibly shrinking! Her shoulders within my encircling arm, melting... palpably dwindling.

Horrible! And there was a great cry from Brett. "Leela! My God, Leela—"

At the horror of it, Brett and I stood dumbly staring; and again the girls clung together. They seemed dizzy; they swayed, almost fell, then steadied themselves, visibly smaller now, like beautifully formed little children, clinging together, no taller than my waist.

Dwindling!

Then Frannie pointed to the thicket. Two small human figures stood there—a foot high, no more. A grinning gnome-like man, with black matted hair on his naked chest; and a woman—a woman thick and shapeless. A foot in height. But they were shrinking very fast. And beside them were four small animals with horns—grotesque like a dream mingling dog and horse and moose. The animals, too, were dwindling.

Brett saw them; but neither he nor I made a move. At our feet Frannie and Leela, no higher than our ankles now, were gazing up at us, with tiny unraised arms, pleading.

"Leela! Frannie!" We knelt by them. Then Brett in an agony of terror lifted Leela in his hand. "Leela! Don't—don't get any smaller!"

Then he put her down. She ran, half fell the distance of my foot to reach Frannie. And I heard Frannie's tiny voice calling up to us in gasps, "We're going! He—that man there with the woman—caught us. Forced—down our throats—a drug. We—going—"

Smaller than my finger. Then so small we knelt to see them.

They were huddled against the side of a pebble. Then they seemed struggling toward the pebble. Behind it. Under it. Under its curve....

Brett cried, "Don't move, Frank! My God, we might trample on them! Don't move!"

The figures in the thicket had vanished. By the pebble which Brett guarded so carefully I thought I saw Leela and Fannie. Saw a movement, as though an ant were there, hiding under the pebble.

Then—they were not visible. We did not dare look too closely. They were gone! Still there within a foot of our straining eyes—but so immeasurably distant! Lost! Gone! Stolen into smallness!

3

THE THING IN THE FOG

Within the arcade, when the alarm had sounded, Martt leaped to his feet, dragging Frannie after him. He saw me knocked to the floor, but could not reach me. A press of panic-stricken people was sweeping him away, but he clung to Frannie. Then he saw me regain my feet; saw me looking around. But I did not see him; and though he shouted at me, in the noise and confusion his words were lost.

Frannie gasped, "What is it? What's the matter, Martt? What is it?"

Martt did not know. But he guessed, and his heart went cold with fear. "We must get outside, Frannie. Hold tight! This way—it's nearer! There goes Frank—we'll join him outside."

Martt was forcing a way for them through the crowd. Frannie stumbled. Her hold on him was broken. She fell; and before he could reach her he was knocked backward by a running man. When he regained his feet a swift-moving group was between him and Frannie. He saw two girls stop and help her up; then discard her. Saw her turn, confused, and run into a space where the crowd was thinner. He was being shoved away from her.

"Fannie! Wait! This way!"

But she did not hear him. And then he could no longer see her; there were too many people in between. He struggled in that direction, then he thought he saw me, and turned momentarily the other way....

Martt found himself alone, outside the arcade. The crowd was thinner. Still he was not certain of the cause of all this panic. Then he saw the giant. Stood, and stared with tumultuously beating heart.

A man bumped into him, for an instant he thought that it was Brett. Memory of Brett reminded him that Brett was probably within the arcade, back of the platform-stage. He saw an opening, there in the arcade wall; he thought it was a doorway, leading back of the stage. He started for it, ran headlong into a girl standing there, staring out over the water to where the giant now had faced about and was wading away.

"Martt!"

"You, Zee! Where's Brett? Where are Leela and your father?"

She clung to him, her draperies drooping, her hair tumbling in great dark waves over her white shoulders as she shook her head.

"I do not know. They were in there a moment ago. Frannie came in—she and Leela were at the other door. Martt—that giant—"

"He's going away, Zee. Look! You see him turned about? Don't be frightened. We must find Brett. I don't know where Frank is—I lost him. There he is—isn't that Frank? Oh—Frank!"

They ran toward a man's figure, passing along a distant line of trees. But when they caught up with it, the man was a stranger. Ahead of them, hidden by a thicket, voices were shouting. A rhythmic call. Martt and Zee listened; but Martt could not understand the shouted words.

"What is it, Zee? Can you understand them?"

"They're saying, 'The messenger from Reaf!' Some messenger from Reaf has come with news."

"Come on. Let's go see what it is."

He gripped her hand. They ran swiftly through the woods.

They were already several hundred feet from the arcade. The lagoon was on its other side; ahead of them was a patch of woods, dark, for the lantern-flowers did not grow along here. And beyond the woods, the shore of the island where the shouting sounded.

They ran. Soon Zee was ahead, leaping like a young chamois, her veils and hair flying.

"Wait!" he called. "Not so fast!"

She stopped abruptly. And Martt stopped There was a pounding on the shore; waves rolling up, as though the peaceful lake were torn by a storm.

"What's that, Zee?" But the shouting began again; and without answering, Zee started ahead.

The starlit lake came into view. Like a distant, monstrous shadow, the retreating giant was visible against the stars. On the shore, white waves were rolling up. A boat was here, with its sail flapping. A wave caught it, turned it over.

On the strand a group of people were standing with the man who had come in this boat from Reaf. Zee joined the group. In a moment she returned.

"He says—the messenger says—that giants are in Reaf! The city is emptied—the people have scattered into the country. The road to Crescent is crowded with people coming here."

"Giants! There—as well as here—"

"Yes. They did not attack. There were two giants. They stood in the lake and laughed while the people fled from the city. Hundreds were killed in the rush to get out—hundreds were swept away into the subterranean rivers and the giants stood and laughed. The city is deserted, and the two giants are there now."

Men were helping the messenger right his boat. The group on the shore scattered back over the island, calling, "Giants! Giants are in Reaf!"

The messenger climbed into his boat, headed it out over the now calmer lake.

Martt and Zee momentarily were alone. He stared at her. He was stunned, confused. Giants, everywhere. This thing that had been worrying Brett for so long had come. Death, everywhere.

"Let's get back, Zee. We must find Brett."

It seemed shorter along the shore—a turn of the island nearby, into the lagoon, and thus back to the arcade. They started off, running again. It was deserted along here. Zee was leading. Suddenly she stopped in full flight, gripped Martt, drew him behind a huge, pot-bellied tree trunk which stood near the water's edge.

"Zee, what—?"

"There, over there."

"Where? I don't see anything." She whispered insistently, "Over there—in that open space. Back from the shore."

She was crouching, and he crouched beside her; followed her gesture with his gaze—and saw what she saw.

Tiny moving figures on the ground. Four of them, small dark blobs against the white sand. They were about a hundred feet away from where Martt and Zee were crouching. They had come out of the woods evidently, and were crossing this patch of white sand, heading for the water. Martt blinked and rubbed his eyes, staring at them. They moved in tiny leaps, bounding soundlessly over the sand. Each of them a foot long perhaps. Strange in shape; animal or human, he could not Say.

"What are they, Zee?"

But she did not answer. Her little body was shrinking against him; he could feel her shudder.

The figures seemed long and thin, horizontal to the ground, with something sticking upright like a tower from the middle of them. Martt gasped. He had thought them four animals, with humps like upright towers. They were not. He saw them now as running dogs with horns, each with a tiny human figure on its back. And he gasped again. They were growing larger! They crossed the sand in bounds and momentarily stopped. Already they were fully half normal size. Four horned animals that might have been grotesque dogs, or horses. Saddled; and mounted upon them, a heavy-set, half-naked man; a strange, shapeless woman—and two girls!

Normal size now! No, already they were larger! Growing rapidly larger! Frannie and Leela!

Martt half started to his feet. He opened his mouth to shout impulsively, but Zee drew him back and silenced him. The four animals were taking to the water. Swimming with heads stretched out. Martt could see Frannie and Leela bending forward, each clutching the horn of her mount. In single file the animals swam swiftly out into the starlit lake. They did not seem to be growing any further. Twice normal size perhaps. Soon they were four dark blobs on the shining water. Visually seeming smaller by distance. V-shaped lines of silver phosphorescence streamed out in the water behind them with their swift forward progress.

And presently they were vanished.

Martt and Zee stood up. They could not explain it. They tried to, but could not. But the main facts were clear. That had been a man and woman giant, and four of their animals, They had captured Frannie and Leela. Had made the girls and the animals change size like themselves. They had all, just now, been very small in size. To escape observation coming across the island to its shore, Martt concluded.

He said, "We must get to Brett—tell him about this. And then—go after them—"

Again they started running along the shore, intending to turn at the lagoon-mouth for the arcade. Martt's thoughts flew swift as his legs. Leela and Frannie captured… they must be rescued… then all of them would get into the vehicle and go to Earth—get out of this danger….

Zee was saying "That is Reaf, off that way where they went."

The wading giant had also gone that way. The messenger had said that Reaf was deserted, that giants were there. Evidently Reaf was the place at which these giants first appeared. Evidently it was the point of entrance and departure for them into and out of this realm. Leela and Frannie were being taken to Reaf….

Martt's heart leaped. An idea was forming in his mind. A plan—a mad, reckless plan. But it seemed possible of success…. He thought of the vehicle. It would be of no use against these giants. It was too unwieldy. Besides, shut up in it one could not attack. And when they stopped it to disembark, the giants would overwhelm it. Or, if at the moment it was too gigantic for them, then they would escape before the occupants of the vehicle could get out to stop them…. And besides, the vehicle was too precious—no chances like that should be taken with it.

Martt told himself that he must get Brett to hide the vehicle. Guard it somehow….

A mad idea, this plan he was pondering…. They came to the lagoon-mouth; and here to crystallize Martt's plan, to make it seem feasible—here lay a small sailboat, deserted by its owner. It lay, half pulled up on the sand, around the bend of the lagoon.

"Zee! Stop! Wait! I want to talk to you."

Zee had been bounding ahead of him. She stopped, waited, faced him. He was breathless.

"That sailboat," he said. "It's one of the fast kind, isn't it?"

"Yes." She regarded it. "Yes. Very fast."

It was no more than a shell. A flat, spoon-shaped affair, with a small cockpit just large enough for two; and it had a very tall, flexible mast, and an overlarge crescent sail. The sail was flapping. Out on the lake the wind had risen. It was blowing directly toward Reaf.

"Zee, listen—could you sail that boat?"

"Oh, yes."

"You could handle it in that wind out there?"

"Yes. Of course."

"And it would go—how fast, Zee?"

"You mean—to Reaf?" She was as excited as he.

"Yes. To Reaf. We could get there. Go after them. Cautiously. We could hide before we got there. I've a plan—"

"How long to Reaf?" She pondered. "Three—what you call hours. We go fast in a wind like that."

"Yes. That's it. Fast. Three hours. Zee, listen. Reaf must be where the giants go to leave for their own world. They're taking Frannie and Leela there. You see? And if we can get there—get into Reaf"—he gestured—"Zee, if they—those giants are very big, then we to them are small. Tiny. And it's quite dark. It would be dark in the caverns near Reaf—the houses there near the subterranean rivers. We would be so small the giants might not see us."

He drew a long breath. "My plan, Zee, is to get in there, hide, and find a giant from whom we can steal the drugs. With the drugs—"

She was trembling with excitement. No fear now. Reckless as only youth can be. "Oh Martt, if we could get the drugs! Brett said the giants must be using drugs. And make ourselves larger than the giants—"

"Yes. Then I can fight them. Rescue Leela and Frannie. We've got to do it. Bring Leela and Frannie safely back. We'll say, 'Here they are, Brett.' But if we wait, if we stop now it will be too late."

Before Martt's eyes was the vision at himself and Zee returning victoriously with the rescued girls. And with the drugs in his possession. There would be no danger then. The giants, knowing the drugs were stolen, would not dare remain.... They would all escape up into their own world.

"Will you do it, Zee? Shall we go?"

"Yes."

Martt thought of his flash-cylinder. "I wish I had it, Zee."

"Where is it?"

"In the vehicle. But we have no time to get it."

"I think it would not be of much use."

"No. I don't think so either. But all I've got is this." He displayed a knife whose blade, as long as his hand, slid back into its handle for a sheath.

"Good," she said. He replaced the knife. They climbed into the boat. Mart shoved it off.

In a moment they were beyond the quiet lagoon, heading out into the starlit Lake, with the lights of the island fading behind them.

The wind was strong when they were beyond the island. The sail bellied out in front of them like a great crescent dish; the spoon-shaped boat, barely skimming the surface of the water, rode high on a white wave beneath it. Zee lay on her side, upraised upon an elbow with her hand on the knife-blade rudder that trailed the water behind them. Beside her, hunched with arms wrapping his upraised knees, Martt sat and peered ahead under the sail.

The lake was dim in the starlight: its concavity rose to the horizon. It seemed empty ahead. No boats. The wading giant had vanished; the swimming figures were gone.

As they sailed with the wind, the night seemed windless and calm, save that the lake boiled under them, swiftly passing. Martt was in no mood to talk. Zee, too, was silent, engrossed with her task of guiding the boat.

Occasionally, with a surreptitious, sidelong glance, Martt regarded her intent little face, earnest and solemn. Long, dark lashes, tendrils of dark hair around the slim white column of her throat; her outstretched limbs revealed by the stirring draperies.... A lock of her hair flew across his cheek. He touched it, cast it away.

"Zee?"

"Yes, Martt?"

"I was thinking—you dance very beautifully."

She turned to him, and smiled; a whimsical smile, and her eyes were dark woodland dells of fairyland. "Father does not think so. A peddler of movement—violent, tempestuous movement! Do you think that, Martt?"

"No," he assured her. "Of course I don't." As she turned back to her steering, his fingers furtively caught a hem of her robe and held it.

There was a long silence. Then he said, as though there had been no silence, "Of course I don't. I think you dance beautifully." And he added, "It made me—" His tongue was about to say, "It made me love you," but his beating heart smothered the words. He amended, "It made me think that your father was very wrong to say that. And about Leela, too."

At the mention of Leela he saw a shadow cross Zee's face. He tensed himself; set his jaw grimly. This was no time for thoughts of love. Leela, and his sister Frannie, were captured by giants. There was work, danger for him and for Zee, up ahead in this starlit night: He would need all his wits, all his resourcefulness....

He remembered the one visit he had formerly made to Reaf; tried to recall how the city lay. Tried to plan what he and Zee would do, now when they got there.

He said, "Zee, the rivers at Reaf that plunge into the mountains—no one has been in them very far?"

"No," she said.

"Can you walk along their banks, inside, under the mountains?"

She nodded. "In some places there are narrow ledges beside the water. But how far—no one knows."

"And in other places—near Reaf, I mean—there are tunnels? Passageways?"

"Yes. Back into the caves and beyond."

"I think," he said, "that back through there is the way to the giants' huge outer world. They've come down, and through the ground behind the mountains. Do you suppose they'll take Leela and Frannie up to their own realm? Or keep them in Reaf?"

"I think—we do not know anything about it," she said.

He smiled grimly. "You're right, we don't. Why the giants should come here at all I don't know. But we're going to know more about it before we get through with them, Zee. What I'm hoping is that we might find one of them alone. We've got to get the drugs away from them somehow. We've got to."

Martt remembered once arguing with Brett about the giants. Brett had thought that they used some drug—two drugs—one to shrink proportionately each of their body cells, and the other similarly to increase the size of the cells. Drugs of the kind had already been sought for on Earth. Nitrogen was the basis for growth. And the new element, Parogen, had been found to cause a shrinkage. In Mars they had developed such drugs further—but they were still impractical for human use.

These giants evidently had something of the kind. And it must be radio-active—it must cause a radiation affecting vegetable or animal matter in near proximity to the changing body. The garments of the giants expanded and contracted with their bodies. But Brett had said that a weapon in your hand—particularly one of mineral—would not change size…. The thought was to some slight degree, at least, comforting to Martt; the giants would be unarmed.

Zee's voice broke in on his thoughts. "Look, there are the mountains behind Reaf."

Over the lake, ahead of them the distant horizon was a haze of phosphorescence. But to the left a line of shore had become visible; and now Martt saw up ahead the vague, dark outlines of the mountains. Sharp, jagged peaks, tinged with a green-white.

Another hour. The shore to the left was nearer. Undulating land along the lake. A ribbon of road along the water…. Martt thought he could see blobs moving along it. Away from Reaf, moving toward Crescent.

"The refugees from Reaf," said Zee. "The messenger said all the roads were crowded."

Another half-hour. Ahead the mountains frowned, rising sheer from the water. The lake was more shallow here; they began passing flat, muddy islands, with river channels flowing between them as in a delta. A blur there, at the foot of the mountains, was Reaf. The silver phosphorescence of the lake was darkening; the water looked muddy, turgid. In a narrow channel between two islands, Martt noticed a quite visible current flowing toward Reaf. It rippled the water as it passed over a bar which Zee skillfully avoided.

There were other islands, with water bubbling up from them, and clouds of steam rising. Zee trailed her hand overboard.

"We are in the warm water now. Feel it, Martt."

The lake water, fed by boiling springs from all this region, was noticeably warmer. And every moment the current toward Reaf was becoming stronger. Martt knew that all this part of the lake converged to the mouths of the subterranean rivers at Reaf; converged and plunged under the ground.

The city of Reaf was now in sight, It spread sidewise over an area of a mile or two. The houses were perched on stilts, like flat, awkward, long-legged birds squatting in the water.

During all this time Martt and Zee had been watching closely for any sign of giants. There were none in sight—nothing that seemed alive over this turgid water, the disconsolate group of houses, the sheer cliffs with the sullen mountains above them. Two yawning black openings showed where the rivers entered....

A deserted city, its inhabitants fled. Some had been drowned, the messenger said. There would be no floating bodies; the current would have sucked them all into those yawning black mouths.... A deserted city. But somewhere in there among the houses, giants might be lurking....

Martt said abruptly, "We'd better get the sail down. They can see it too easily." They were still some two miles from the outskirts of the city. But no more than half a mile from the nearer shore. It swung past them to the left; perpendicular black cliffs rising from the water with a narrow rocky strip along the bottom against which the water sucked.

Zee helped Martt lower the sail. There were poles aboard; the lake here was no more than five feet deep. They could pole the boat ashore. Walk unobserved toward the nearer river-mouth. Into the city, to hide among its buildings.

With a thrill of apprehension Martt realized that they might already have been seen. But he thought it unlikely. From the hot water, vapor was rising in a fog. It hung like a white shroud over Reaf. Once in it, surrounded by the fog, they would be comparatively safe.

"Zee, can you swim?"

"Oh, yes," she said. "But Martt, if you get in the water, be very careful of the rivers."

Silently they poled the boat to shore. Drew it up from the current, left it on a shelving rock ledge. The strip here was some ten feet wide; the hot, black lake in front, sluggishly surging toward Reaf; and above them the smooth cliff-face.

The wind had turned—a swirling current turned by the mountains. The fog from Reaf came rolling down upon them. It grew dark; the stars were obscured. In the humid steam they could see no more than twenty feet.

"Good," said Martt. "This is what we want." He spoke in a half-whisper; stoutly, but his heart was beating fast. He drew his knife and opened its blade. "Come on, Zee. And listen, you keep close to me. Whatever happens, we must keep together. And if you see anything—or hear anything—don't speak. Just touch my arm."

They started, creeping silently along the rocks in the fog. It seemed miles. The water was hot beside them. The fog, like a gray curtain, opened reluctantly before their advance. Presently the ghostly outlines of houses were visible, a group of them clinging forlornly together near the shore. Wooden platforms like balconies connected them. A bridge came over and down to the rocks.

Then other buildings. A large one of two stories, backed against the cliff-face. Martt and Zee went under it, groping in the blackness among its piling. The close, heavy air smelt of fish.

They came out to find that the rocky shore had ended. A narrow incline walk led out and up over the water to another group of ghostly buildings. They were some thirty feet away, standing on stilts some ten feet high. In the gray darkness of the fog their shadowy outlines were barely visible.

Martt stopped. "Zee," he whispered, "how far are we from the nearest river-mouth?"

"Not far," she said. "Listen."

In the silence he heard the rush of water. As he stood there, suddenly this whole adventure seemed impractical. There were no giants here. They had all gone on, up into largeness unfathomable, taking Leela and Frannie with them. How could he follow? Even if he dared plunge under the mountains, he could never reach that outer realm. It was gigantic—compared to his present size it might be a million miles away.

Or, if there were giants still lurking here in Reaf, of what use to seek them out and be killed by them?

For an instant Martt hopelessly considered turning back. But he never reached the decision; Zee's fingers gripped his arm—cold, shuddering fingers. He stared, as he saw her staring, and within him his blood seemed to stop its flow.

Something was coming down the narrow incline bridge at the foot of which Martt and Zee were standing frozen, transfixed with horror. Something... in all the dark murk of fog Martt could not make it out. An animal? It seemed oblong, the size of a large dog. He could see its moving legs—eight or ten legs, moving as it walked. He felt Zee stir beside him; he withstood his impulse to run. That would make too much noise; the thing would bound after them—catch them....

There was a rotting post beside Zee. She and Martt crouched

there and watched with a horrified fascination the thing as it came padding down the incline. It was vaguely green-white; it seemed luminous. As it approached, Martt saw it was a sleek body, moving lithe like a panther. A green-white thing. And then he saw that it was headless. A blunt end, with a gaping, dripping mouth and a shining green eye on a protruding stalk. It stopped, turned the eye to look upward and back.

Martt's breath was stopped. In the silence he seemed to hear his own tumultuously beating heart, and Zee's. The thing was coming on again. Now Martt could hear sounds from it. A whining; a babbling. And from the houses, up there at the end of the incline, came another sound. A great, heavy breathing. A giant was up there asleep! This thing—like nothing of Zee's world—belonged to the giants! Martt's heart, for all his horror, leaped with exultation. A giant, asleep! A giant smaller in size now, if he were up in those houses. He would have the drugs; they could steal the drugs from him while he slept.

The thing on the incline was quite close. It glowed with its own light, greenly phosphorescent, like the ghost of something in a dream, leprous with its missing head.

Another moment. It was passing close beside Martt. A luminous liquid dripping from the gaping slit of its mouth. Its eye on the stalk peered ahead. Its voice was clearly audible. A whine; and babbling sounds like words.

Revulsion, even more than fear, swept Martt. This thing was muttering words! Animal, or human—it was talking, babbling to itself. Strange words of an unknown tongue—but human words. Babbling them as though with reason unhinged. Gruesome! This leprous thing—leprous of body; and leprous of mind!

It passed within an arm's length of Martt as he crouched. And suddenly, without conscious thought, he struck at it with his naked knife. Horrible! The knife sank, but the thing was scarce ponderable! Martt's hand with the knife went down and through the luminous green body, with a feeling of warmth and a wet stickiness, but no more.

The force of the blow, unresisted, threw Martt off his balance. He fell forward, but still clutched the knife. The thing, with a sharp, horrible cry of pain, lurched backward. Then stood with its eye quivering, poised for its attack.

4

THE WILD NIGHT RIDE

Frannie forced her way out of the crowded arcade, with its struggling, panic-stricken occupants. She was confused, terrified. Separated from me, and then from Martt, her only idea was to find us again; or find Brett. Outside the arcade she turned aimlessly to where the crowd momentarily was least dense. Panic-stricken people—all strangers. Then she saw Leela in the shadow of a doorway of the arcade, and ran to her.

"Leela! What is it? What has happened?"

People around them were shouting. Leela said, "Giants. There is a giant off there in the lake. I was looking for Brett. He came out here. Oh, Frannie—"

The two girls clung to each other. It was dark where they stood. At the moment the crowd had surged the other way. Suddenly Frannie became aware of a dark form looming beside her. A man twice the size of herself. She tried to scream, but a great palm went over her face. She felt herself being jerked from her feet....

She half fainted; recovered to find herself in a thicket within a few feet of the arcade. Leela was beside her. Leela panted, "Don't scream, Frannie! They'll—kill us if we scream!"

The man was with them, and a thick-set lump of a woman. Not so large now. Almost normal in size, for they were dwindling. The man was naked to the waist, a gray-white, barrel-like chest matted with hair. A face, fearsome with menacing eyes, and a head of matted black locks.

And in the thicket were four horned animals; saddled, like large horses with spreading antlers. The animals were dwindling....

The man rasped a command at Leela. From his belt he drew small pellets white like tiny pills of medicine. He thrust one at Leela, forced it down her throat. Leela gasped, "You must take it, Frannie. He says—it is harmless—but if we resist—he will kill."

Then the man thrust his fingers into Frannie's mouth, his arm holding her roughly. She gulped, swallowed. It was an acrid taste....

The man pushed her roughly from the thicket. And pushed Leela. His triumphant laugh was the rasp of a file on metal. Leela and Frannie stumbled to the wall of the arcade, stood clinging together. And suddenly, with the realization of what was upon her, Leela screamed. And Frannie screamed, though she did not yet understand.

A wave of nausea possessed Frannie. Her head was reeling. Voices sounded near by—familiar men's voices. My voice, and Brett's! We came running at the sound of the screams.

Frannie held tight to the swaying Leela as Brett and I rushed up. And I took Frannie in my arms. Brett was demanding, "Leela, what is it? You're not hurt, are you? What is it?"

Frannie wanted to try and tell me. "Frank—oh—" She choked; her throat was constricted.

And then Frannie really knew! Within my arms she felt herself shrinking! Growing smaller; but it was not so much that; rather was it that my encircling arm was expanding, holding her more loosely.

With the horror of it, Brett and I stood apart. Frannie's nausea was passing, her head was steadier, but dizzy with the strange movement of the scene around her. She clung to Leela, and, of everything within her vision, only Leela was unchanging. The wall of the arcade was slowly passing upward; its nearer corner was moving slowly away; Brett and I were growing. Our waists reaching to Frannie's head; and then our knees. She gazed upward to where fifteen or twenty feet above her, our horrified faces stared down.

The mind always takes its personal viewpoint. Frannie and Leela were dwindling into smallness. But now that the nausea and dizziness were past, to them, they alone were normal. Everything else seemed changing… the whole scene, growing gigantic….

It was a slow, crawling growth—a steady, visible movement. The ground beneath their feet was a fine white sand. To Frannie's sight this patch of sand had originally been some ten feet, with the arcade wall on one aide, and a thicket on the other. But the ground was shifting outward with herself as a center. Under her bare feet she could feel its steady movement—drawing outward, shifting so that her feet were drawn apart. She had to move them constantly.

Beside her now she saw my foot and ankle as large as herself; the towering shafts of my legs—my face a hundred feet or more above her. The arcade wall stretched up almost out of sight—lantern-flowers loomed up there like great colored suns…. The thicket was a hundred feet away—a tangle of jungle.

Then Frannie saw the giant Brett reach down and pick Leela up on his hand—saw Leela whirled gasping into the air. A moment, then Brett set her gently back on the ground She was some twenty feet from Frannie. She ran, half stumbled across the rough white ground until again the girls were together.

The arch of my sandaled foot was now as tall as Fannie. The arcade wall was very distant; the thicket was a blur in the

The GIANT WORLD

RAY CUMMINGS

Frannie struggled in the grip of the blood-red, vegetable thing.

distance. That small patch of white sand had unrolled to a great stony plain. Rough; yellow-white stones strewn everywhere. Frannie saw my feet and Brett's—as large as the arcade once had been—moving away with great surging bounds up into the air and back. A boulder was near by—a rock as tall as Frannie. It was visibly growing. She gripped Leela—together they crept to the boulder's side, huddled there.

But they could not remain still The boulder was expanding. It towered over them; but it was drawing away as well, for the ground was expanding. Constantly they shifted their position to remain close to it, to huddle under its protecting curve. It had been a rock taller than their heads; it was now a mountain. It loomed above them—a bulging cliff-face of naked, ragged rock.

Then it was no longer moving. Everything now had steadied; the ground was motionless. A normality came to Leela and Frannie. Their terror faded into apprehension, and a desire, a determination to do what they could to help themselves. They stood up and looked around them.

They were in the midst of a vast, rock-strewn plain, illumined by a half twilight. It seemed miles in extent—a rolling country of naked rock over which, for a sky, hung a remote murk of distance. A naked landscape, rolling upward to a circular horizon, with the circular mountain of rock standing beside them at its center.

Leela now seemed quite calm. She said, "We are not unfathomably small. Too small for Brett to see us, but not if he gets a glass to magnify. He will mark the spot where we are—he will do something, Frannie—we must not be too much frightened."

There seemed nothing that they could do to help themselves. No use to wander; though no great harm either, for they could roam for miles over this rocky waste to cover no more than a foot or two of the white sand Brett would be guarding.

To Frannie's imagination came the thought of insects! A crawling ant in that white sand would now be a monster gigantic! She gazed around in terror, but there was nothing of the kind in sight.

A desolate landscape, empty of movement. Frannie's heart leaped. In the distance something was moving! She gripped Leela.

"There's something out there—something moving out there!"

Tiny moving specks. Too terrified to run, the girls stood staring. A mile or two away, specks were moving across the rocky plain. They seemed coming nearer. They separated into four specks. Four gray blobs, coming swiftly forward.

In a few moments they were distinguishable. Four running animals, bounding, leaping over the rocks. Animals with horns. Two of them running free; two with riders.

Leela gasped, "That's the giant! And the woman! They're coming to find us!"

For a moment the two girls stood transfixed, heedless that they would be discovered. To Frannie came the thought: The giant, the woman and the four animals had been dwindling. They had stood in the thicket, hiding from Brett. They were coming from the thicket now, riding over the vast rocky plain headlong to regain their captives. Brett could not see them; they were too small, Brett was probably standing a few feet from here on the sand—afraid to come closer for fear of treading upon the girls; and those few feet were miles away across this naked desert.

The four animals came leaping forward. They ran low to the ground, necks extended like huge dogs an a trail. Already they were no more than half a mile away. The figures of the riding man and woman showed plainly. They all seemed about normal size as compared to Frannie and Leela.

Abruptly Frannie recovered her wits. "We must hide! They must not find us!"

They hid, out of sight around a corner of the lower rock-face of the mountain; crouched, waiting with wildly beating hearts.

But it was useless. Either they had been seen or the animals scented them. Soon they heard the man calling his mount. No noise of galloping hoofs, for the beasts ran lightly on padded feet. A moment, then the animals burst into view around the jutting rock; bounded up and stopped before the crouching girls.

The man dismounted. His grin was a leer of triumph. He spoke to Leela—a harsh, guttural command in her own language, as he had spoken before when he forced the drug upon her.

Leela dragged herself to her feet, and Frannie after her. The man spoke again. Less harshly this time, and at greater length. He gestured at Frannie.

Leela said, with a quiver in her voice that she tried to hold to calmness, "He tells me that his name is Rokk. This woman here is his mate—he calls her Mobah. He says they come from a very big world—down here to our world of infinite smallness. Oh, Frannie, what can we do? He says they are going to take us with them, up there to that Giant World."

Frannie, too, strove for calmness. "Ask him—why? What harm have we done to him? Tell him—we don't want to go—"

Leela turned to this man who had called himself Rokk. Then she appealed to the woman—but the woman stared dumbly and turned away.

"Frannie—he says we will learn later what he wants. He says—we will not be harmed if we cause no trouble. We are going—he says he is going to take us—"

"Which way?" Frannie interrupted.

"I don't know. I suppose to Reaf."

"Ask him."

Leela asked him. "Yes, by way of Reaf. He says we will mount the animals—he calls them dhranes. They run very swiftly—as Brett describes your wolves of the northern ice-fields of your Earth."

Frannie demanded, "He says we go to Reaf?"

"Yes. We will cross the island—out the lagoon—riding the dhranes as they swim."

Memory of the island—the arcade—the lagoon and the lake

came to Frannie. The island! It seemed so remote, so gigantic. This vast rocky waste surrounding them now was only a small patch of white sand beside the arcade wall.

She said swiftly, "Leela, ask him how we can ever do that when we are so small? Why, it must be hundreds of miles—for us in this size—just to reach the shore of the island."

"I told him that. He said, 'Of course.' He said he has been riding from the thicket ever since he got small enough to avoid Brett's sight. While they were still diminishing they were riding. He was afraid Brett would see them—but he had to take that chance."

"I mean," said Frannie breathlessly, "tell him we must get larger. It is too far in this small size. Tell him you know the island and the lake well—we will help him escape—"

Leela nodded eagerly. "So that if we get large, Brett may see us?"

"Yes. Try and get him to make us large at once—now. Tell him we'll help him—"

Rokk grinned sardonically at Leela's words. Leela turned to Frannie in chagrin.

"He says he will do as he thinks best—and we will do as we are told."

Rokk added another command. Leela said, "We must mount the dhranes, Frannie. I think we had better do as he says—and not talk. Can you ride a saddle like that?"

From Fannie's viewpoint, the dhranes were now about the size of small horses—four-legged, long-haired, shaggy beasts with crooked, wide-spreading antlers. They moved as though on springs. Frannie was reminded by their movements of giant leopards she had seen in cages on Earth. But they seemed gentle, docile enough. The saddles were oblong, padded with fur, with a high and a low foot-rail, both upon the same side, on which the rider's feet could rest.

"I can ride that," said Frannie; and nimbly mounted. There was no bridle; Frannie leaned forward and clutched the antlers. Leela mounted. Rokk moved his dhrane about by spoken words, and by slapping its haunches with his hands.

Leela said, "He is going to give us some of the drug, Frannie. Some now—to make us larger. But before we are very large he says we will be beyond the arcade, in the woods where Brett can not see us. We will ride very fast—"

The animals lapped their drug eagerly. The man and woman took theirs, with Leela and Frannie. To Frannie again came a moment of nausea—a reeling of the senses. But it was quickly passed.

Rokk shouted. Frannie tensed herself. The dhrane under her bounded forward. The ride began.

At first Frannie clung tensely to the antlers; but soon she found it was not necessary to do so. The dhrane ran with long, smooth bounds; sure-footed on the rocks as a chamois, noiseless, lithe as a great cat. It ran, with head extended, low to the ground; beneath her, Frannie could feel the play of its smooth muscles, rippling under its shaggy skin.

The woman Mobah rode her dhrane behind Frannie. Leela was directly ahead, with Rokk leading. In single file they bounded forward. Leela's black hair and draperies flew in the wind. She rode, bending forward, her body loosely responsive to the animal's bounds.

The wind of their forward movement sang in Frannie's ears. The ground fled by under her with a blur of yellow movement. And all around her was the murky night, rushing at her, passing, and closing in behind.

A wild, night ride like the fairy dream of a child. Wild, and free... a fairy dream....

An exaltation was upon Frannie; she urged her mount to greater speed. And thought of the drug she had taken....

The drug was acting. The rushing night seemed shrinking. Everywhere the murk was contracting. The ground was smoothing and turning from its yellow to white. Overhead a remote—very remote—spot of red light shone like a dying sun in the heavens. A lantern-flower! Frannie's heart leaped with triumph. They were growing larger....

She heard Rokk shout to his dhrane; felt her own mount stretch closer to the ground as the speed was increasing. The rushing night contracting... they seemed riding up... and up... the ground, the night was shrinking under them....

A wild, night ride up through a fairy's dream... it seemed endless. Wildly free, with the exaltation of a child's fancy upon it....

Frannie became aware that the vast rocky plain was shrunken to a smoother level. And ahead now, she saw a great forest, with colored suns about it. Soon they were in the forest. A jungle. Flat, orange stalks of grass twenty feet high. The dhranes bounded through them. Shaggy outlines of tree trunks, each vast as a mountain. They rose into unfathomable murky distance overhead. But these were all dwindling. The giant jungle was shrinking... passing slowly, but ever faster.

A fantasy... the dream of a child....

Rokk called again. Their pace slackened. Frannie saw an open space ahead. Coarse white sand—a patch of it half a mile in extent. Beyond it a broad beach. Water shining off there. The lake, with stars above it.

The dhranes ran more slowly. The white open space shrank as they traversed it. The beach rushed at them. It had narrowed. Frannie saw it as almost of normal—aspect the narrow shore of the island. The lake was starlit—beautiful.

Rokk paused a moment at the water's edge. Frannie gazed around. The woods were behind them. A large, dark tree-trunk was nearby on the shore. Frannie gazed that way idly; and though she did not know it, Martt and Zee were crouching there, staring with a confused fascination. A moment. The shore shrunk further; the water had advanced to lap the stamping, impatient feet of the dhranes. Rokk spoke softly. His dhrane waded in, with the others following.

Frannie again gripped her beast's horns. The water rose almost to the saddle. It was warm and pleasant. The dhrane swam smoothly, swiftly, with neck stretched out, nose skimming the surface.

A dwindling silver lake. Ripples of silver-green phosphorescence; line of silver fire diverging behind the swimming animals....

Frannie turned to gaze at the receding island. An island already shrunken, dotted with shrinking colored lights. And ahead, the empty starlit lake.

Riding over the land, it had been a breathless whistling of wind, a swift surging of the ground beneath Frannie's feet. Here in the lake it was quiet and calm; the warm lapping of the silver-streaked water; the quiet stars overhead. Frannie heard Rokk talking back over his shoulder to Leela, and then Leela drew in her mount and spoke to Frannie.

"He says the giants have all gone back through Reaf to their own world. One was wading out here toward Reaf. He was very large then; he is to stay in Reaf on guard, while we go on. He is there now—it is not far."

"How big are we, Leela? Did he say?" There was no way, here in the lake, by which size could be compared. The exaltation of the ride—its swift, tempestuous movement—the wild, romantic fantasy of it—all this was leaving Frannie. A depression was upon her. She added, "Oh, Leela, Brett did not see us! And Frank—will we ever see them again?"

Leela said, "We are about twice normal size—it will not be far to Reaf, swimming like this." In the starlight, Frannie could see that Leela was smiling; a wistful, heavy-hearted smile. She was trying to be brave. And Frannie smiled back.

"We mustn't get frightened, Leela. Just watch our chance—try to escape. You stay by me all you can. I mean—when we get"—there was a catch in her voice—"when we get—under the mountains beyond Reaf."

Leela nodded. Rokk was calling, and Leela urged her dhrane forward.

Soon the left-hand shore and the mountains ahead were visible. The water grew warmer. Small islands appeared. The dhranes panted with the heat of the water; in the muddy channels between the islands, sometimes they floundered. Steam was in the air; ahead it lay like a bank of fog, with the frowning mountains rising above it.

Presently, through the fog, the houses of Reaf came into view. Small ghostly outlines of houses on stilts. To the right of them was a yawning black mouth where one of the rivers plunged into the mountain. The turgid current was swinging that way; Rokk urged the dhrane across it, to the left.

Soon they were swimming among the houses. These seemed very small. Frannie reached up from the dhrane's back and laid her hand on the roof of one as she passed it. Rokk was heading inshore. The mountain here was a frowning cliff-face, with a very narrow ledge at the water level. The ledge ended in a wooden incline bridge leading upward to a group of buildings near shore. Six or eight small houses with doors and rectangles of windows, clustered there together, perched on stiff wooden legs over the water. The incline bridge connected them with the shore, and they were strung together by a broad wooden platform.

Rokk shouted, and from behind the buildings a giant appeared. He had been sitting in the water. He stood up, with mud and slime dripping from him. A man, like Rokk, but younger. His hair was sleek and black, and fell long to his bared chest, across which a skin was draped. His face was broad and flat, and hairless. He stood with the water to his knees, beside the buildings with his arm arched over their roofs as he leaned against them.

He smiled. He called, "Ae, Rokk!" And Rokk answered, "Ae, Degg."

They spoke together. Then they spoke in Leela's language. Leela murmured to Frannie, "This man Degg is to remain here until we are safely above."

Rokk issued his commands. Degg sat down again in the water, waist-deep, with his arms holding his hunched-up knees. He yawned and waved his hand as Rokk swam his dhrane away.

Again in single file, they swam. As they passed the buildings Frannie chanced to glance up. On the porch-like platform up there she caught a glimpse of a green-white shape—a thing stretched out somnolent—a thing, headless!

It was only a glimpse. Frannie's swimming dhrane carried her beyond sight of it.… She was shuddering.

The water now was unpleasantly hot. The current was strong. It was beginning to ripple the water. Ugly, white ripples… sinister.

The dhranes swam with the moving water. But they tossed their heads, uneasy.… Rokk was continually shouting, forcing his mount forward.

There were no houses here. The cliff-face was moving swiftly past. And then a black mouth swept into view. A hundred feet high and twice as broad. A mouth, with steam like the fetid breath of a monster....

The water was sweeping that way. Surging in a torrent. White water, leaping over jagged rock-points that split it into foam....

And from the mouth came a sullen roaring....

Frannie's dhrane lifted its head with a sharp bleat of fear. Its body was swung sidewise by the tumbling water, but it recovered and swam desperately.

The roaring rose to a deafening torrent of sound. White water was leaping everywhere. Frannie half closed her eyes; she could see a whirling blob which was Leela ahead of her. Then the black mouth opened to encompass the world as Frannie was swept into it.

An inferno of roaring blackness....

5

CLIMBING INTO LARGENESS UNFATHOMABLE

In the fog and darkness at the foot of the incline, Martt stood tense, with upraised knife. The green-white thing was poised for its leap. It was not babbling now; its eye on the stalk glared balefully. A shudder swept Martt, as Frannie had shuddered an hour before when she and Leela passed this way, and she had caught a glimpse of this thing lying somnolent on the platform above.

Martt muttered, "Stay back, Zee." And then the headless thing leaped. Martt caught it on his out-flung hand and knife, but did not stop it. He felt his hand sinking within it—a soft, sticky warmth. Its body came on, and struck his chest—a blow as though a soft, yielding pillow had struck him.

There was a moment, there in the darkness, of unutterable horror as Martt felt and saw his body mingled with the body of this gleaming thing clawing at him. He struck wildly, fighting, kicking in a panic of futility. Wet, warm and sticky! He seemed to tear its body apart. But the glowing, lurid outlines, wavering, came back always into shape.

The thing itself was in a panic. Lunging, twisting. Its claws scraped Martt's face, too imponderable to scratch. The slit of its month opened to grip his throat; its teeth sank impotently within his flesh. Pressing against him... the slime of it was warm, with a stench, noisome....

Horrible! A nausea made Martt reel. And the thing now

was crying with terrible, frightened cries But they were low, suppressed.

Martt staggered. And suddenly the lurid green shape gathered itself and fled. Martt saw a quivering dark wound in its side. It fled whimpering along the rocks of the shore and disappeared.

Martt relaxed. He was unhurt. He stooped to the water and washed the stickiness from him. He felt a wild, hysterical desire to laugh.

"Zee, it—that thing was as frightened as I was!"

"Are you all right, Martt? It's gone! What was it?" She clutched at him anxiously.

"Yes—all right. It couldn't hurt me and I couldn't hurt it. Not much." He laughed again but suddenly sobered. "Zee, there's a giant up there asleep. Hear him?"

They listened. From up there in the fog the deep, heavy breathing still sounded. Martt whispered, "You wait here, Zee. I'll creep up on him—get the drugs." He turned to her tensely. "Zee, you stay here. Close against the rocks. Whatever happens, you stay here. I'll—If I get the drugs—I'll make myself very large. Kill him—then I'll come back to you. Don't move—whatever happens.

He left her. The wooden incline sloped sharply upward. The fog momentarily seemed clearing. Martt saw above him the outlines of the houses, a broad platform connecting them. And stretched the length of the platform was the huge, recumbent figure of a man. He seemed about forty feet tall. He lay hunched, cramped for space, with one arm up-flung to the roof of a house, and one leg dangling nearly to the water.

Martt reached the platform. He crept past the giant's legs. The waist, wrapped in a skin, was rising and falling with the giant's breathing. Martt's own breath was held. His heart was thumping wildly. The giant stirred, Martt stepped nimbly aside to avoid the movement of the great body.

At the giant's waist he paused, reached up, fumbling. There seemed a belt here, with pockets. The drugs should be there. The bulge of the giant's middle was nearly as high as Martt's chest as he stood upright. He reached up, and over, feeling with careful fingers.

With a thrill of triumph, Martt found two cylinders, each as long as his forearm. In the starlight he opened them, drew from each a flat, square tablet of compressed powder. The drugs! But which was for growth and which for shrinkage? One was larger than the other. It suggested growth. It was flat and square—the length of Martt's thumb. Impulsively he would have crushed it in his mouth and swallowed it. But a thought gave him pause. This giant was nearly seven times larger than himself. This expanded dose of the drug then would be too great. Martt bit off a corner of the white tablet. Swallowed it. An acrid taste…. He replaced the remainder in the cylinder and put both cylinders in his pocket, tying his jacket close around them. Would they expand with his body? He could only hope so.

Expand? How did he know but that he had taken the wrong drugs? Well, he could soon rectify that…. A panic swept Martt that the giant might awaken too soon…. The drug was taking effect; Martt was sick and dizzy. He reeled to a post at an outer corner of the platform. Clung there. He all but slipped and fell into the water ten feet below.

A moment, then the sickness passed. He was growing! He could feel the post shrinking within his grip. The outlines of the houses were contracting. The knife in his hand, already tiny, slipped and fell into the water with a splash.

The post soon was too small for Martt to hold. He reached

over and steadied himself upon the grass roof of the nearest house. It was melting under his hands. The sleeping giant lay at his feet, a giant no longer, a man, like himself—the two of them crowding a tiny, flimsy platform with toy houses beside it, and black water flowing sluggishly close underneath.

A sense of power swept Martt. A triumph. He was not afraid of this man, unarmed like himself. Already the man was undersized…. Why, Martt could grip him, choke him!… These toy houses—a sweep of Martt's arm would have scattered them. Martt was bending awkwardly over the roof-tops. A ripping, tearing noise sounded. The platform, the house, quivered, wavered, collapsed! The whole structure, bending beneath the weight of the two huge bodies, gave way. Martt found himself floundering in warm, muddy water, entangled in a debris of splintered wood and grasslike house-roofs.

And with him, his antagonist, awakened to a startled confusion, floundering, struggling to get upon his feet.

Martt rose to his knees. The shallow lake bottom was sticky with mud. A house-roof hung upon his shoulder. He heaved it off; stood upright, dripping, breathless. The other man was up also. In the starlight, amid the floating wreckage, they faced each other. Martt was the taller; and he was still growing. He saw his enemy shrinking before him. A slim young fellow, with long black hair. A broad, flat face, with a startled surprise on it.

Martt laughed. And shouted, "I've got you now!" He would have leaped. But abruptly he recalled Zee, tiny in size, huddled there by the shore. A lunge of his body—or of this other man's body—a flip of one of these torn housebeams—and Zee would be killed….

Martt turned and waded rapidly away. He wondered if the other man would follow him. Martt wanted to get him farther out into the lake. It was an error; for as Martt turned to look back, he saw his antagonist's hand go to his belt, and then to his mouth. More of the drug! Martt thought that he had in his own pocket all there was of it here. But the giant had more. Already he was growing. As Martt stood undecided, he saw the giant growing like himself. He was smaller than Martt now, but growing more swiftly. He stood for an instant with his arms up-flung toward the stars; then he came wading forward.

The mountains were at Martt's right hand. Shrinking, swiftly contracting. The water now came not much over his ankles; a small patch of wreckage marked where the collapsed buildings had stood.

Martt retreated slightly; he turned, moved to the cliff-face with his back against it.

Then, with a swirl of water, his enemy rushed at him. Martt met the rush unyielding. They locked. Swaying, struggling each to throw other. The lake at their ankles was lashed white. They fought silently grimly. The fellow was strong; he pushed Martt backward against the mountain. His hands strove for Martt's throat. But Martt ripped them away. With a body-hold he bent his adversary backward; but always he could feel the man's body swelling within his grasp.

A desperation seized Martt. If he could not win now, at once, he would lose. This fellow was growing too large. Beside them, as they swayed, Martt caught a glimpse of the mountain. It was now a cliff not much higher than his head. At his feet Martt was dimly aware of a small black hole in the cliff into which water was rushing.

One of Martt's legs was wrapped around the legs of his adversary; and suddenly the man tipped. They went down together, Martt on top, It was like falling into a puddle of water. They lunged, rolled over. And then the giant rose, with Martt clinging to him. He was much larger than Martt now; he heaved himself upward, flung Martt against the cliff. Martt's head and shoulders went over its top. Jagged spires of rock; loose rocks lying there. The giant jerked Martt back; he fell on his feet; saw his antagonist towering over him.

But in Martt's hand now was a jagged lump of rock which he had snatched from the cliff. He flung it, and it caught the giant full on the forehead. He staggered, and as his grip on Martt loosened, Martt leaped away.

And the giant came crashing down, his huge body falling before the hole in the mountain; blocking it so that the surging lake backed up with a deepening torrent of the hot, black water.

Martt stood panting in the starlight. He had won. The scene around him was still dwindling, but in a moment it stopped. Cliffs to his shoulder. A shrunken, shallow lake. Its tiny flat islands were no bigger then his foot. Along its shore where the cliff ended he could see the open country. Tiny threads of roads. An island with points of colored light—the island of the festival. At his feet, miniature houses on stilts, many of them strewn on the water, trampled by this combat of giants in which he had been victorious.

And the fallen giant there in the water, blocking the river mouth, the water deepening against his side.

Martt took a cautious step. Zee was down there somewhere. Then he saw her figure, dimly, in the mist which hung over the lake at his ankles. She seemed about the size of his finger. She was standing at the water's edge, waving up to him.

He bent down—carefully. He said softly, "I see you, Zee. You must get larger. I'll give you some of the drug to take."

She shouted, "Yes." It was a very tiny voice, echoing from far away.

Martt's jacket had been partly torn from him. One of his

shoulders was bare, bleeding from where he had been thrown against the cliff-top. He stooped and dashed water upon the wound; and saw Zee crouch and shield herself from the deluge of water he splashed.

He thought, "Careful, Martt," and from his pocket drew one of the cylinders. The tablets of the drug still were the size of his thumb. He took one, laid it carefully at the water's edge, near Zee. It was nearly the size of her body. She walked to it, examine it.

"Break it," he said. "Eat some—about the size of your thumb."

He could hardly have seen a speck of it so small. Zee found a loose rock. She pounded at the white tablet. Ate a fragment. And presently Martt gave her some of the other drug to stop her growth; and she was his own size, standing beside him gazing at the shrunken scene in wonderment.

They stood consulting over what they should do. They had the precious drugs. Should they return with them to Brett, or go on and rescue Frannie and Leela? Martt was confident. With the drugs in his pocket, all sense of fear was passed. It was obvious that the world here was in no danger. This fallen giant at their feet was the last. But Fannie and Leela were captured; were taken up to that other realm. To delay following would be most dangerous of all.

And Zee agreed. Her eyes were sparkling. She stretched out her white arms. She said, "With this power we would be cowards to turn back—"

The giant still had some of the drugs about his person. Martt bent over him.

"Zee! He isn't dead!"

The young giants face was white; blood was on his forehead where the rock had struck. He opened his eyes; rolled over in the water. The dammed river surged again into its black hole.

"Zee, look! He isn't dead!"

He sat up; smiled in a daze, struggled to rise to his feet but could not.

The rock which Martt had hurled lay like a great boulder in the lake. Martt seized it, but Zee caught his wrist.

"Martt! Don't—"

A sense of shame struck at Mart; he dropped the rock. "Zee, can you talk to him—try if he understands your language."

She spoke, and the young giant answered. He was trying to smile, grateful for the words. Zee stooped and splashed water on his wounded forehead.

"Martt, he says his name is Degg—he has seen Leela and Frannie—a man and woman took them into the river mouth."

The fellow did not seem greatly hurt. He was frightened, watchful, but docile enough. Martt took the drugs from him. "Ask him the way up to his world—it will help us—"

It was the one thing that would help them! Martt realized it.

Degg, outwardly at least, seemed friendly enough. When Zee promised that they would not hurt him—would take him to his own world, the only way he would ever get there, since he had no drugs—he agreed readily to lead them.

"But we must be careful," said Martt. "Never let him get larger than ourselves. And watch him, always."

At Degg's direction, first they diminished their stature until, compared to the buildings of Reaf, they were about fifty feet tall. Degg said, in Zee's language, "We wade now into the black river. Rokk likes to swim—but wading is easier."

They were ready to start. Soon they would be beyond this world—up into largeness unfathomable. Martt said, "We must leave some message for Brett. Let him know what became of us."

There was no way to leave a written message. Conspicuously on a rock near the shore, Martt left the broad belt of his jacket. As he turned away, Degg was calling softly, "Ae! Eeff! Eeff, come here!" The green-white, headless thing was lurking among the rocks. "Eeff, come here!"

It advanced, whimpering. Compared to Martt's fifty-foot stature it seemed now no bigger than a rat. Martt conquered his aversion and stood waiting while it approached. In the star-light it glowed unreal; its eye on the stalk pointed distrustfully at Martt. It stood at Degg's feet; whimpering—and mumbling words.

Degg said to Zee, "It is afraid of your man. I tell it you will do no harm. It wants to come with us." He stooped over. "Eeff; you come with us?"

It understood, partly the words spoken in Zee's language, and partly the gesture. It said mouthingly, "Yes, Eeff come—with you."

Uncanny! Horrible! Martt shuddered. Degg was saying, "It is a very good friend to me. May we take it?"

"All right," said Martt shortly, when Zee translated. But it worried him. He resolved more than ever to watch Degg care-fully, and to watch this headless thing Degg called a friend.

They fed a small morsel of the drug to Eeff, until it had grown to a size normal to them. Then they started. The black mouth of the river, to them in this size, seemed a passageway ten or twelve feet high and twice as broad. The river swirled about their legs; hot, with steam rising. Soon they were in darkness, following the river around a bend. But only for a moment. Martt and Zee were hand in hand. Degg was in advance; Martt could just distinguish Degg's figure with the shining blob of Eeff in the water beside him.

Darkness. But Martt's eyes were growing accustomed to it.

And now the rocks of the caverns seemed to be giving light—a dim phosphorescence. The cavern expanded. They waded across a broad, shallow lake where the water was calm. Then again into a tunnel. Miles down its tortuous course with the river swirling and tumbling about them.

Sometimes there was a dry ledge upon which they could walk. Sometimes the river deepened, and they had to swim. Always Degg advanced grimly, steadily, and silently. A foreboding grew upon Martt. Were they going right? Was this the way Frannie and Leela had gone? Once he whispered, "Do you think, Zee, that he's tricking us?"

She shook her head. "You have all the drugs. He would not dare."

They had waded for hours. Then ahead of them they saw Degg pause. The river here plunged straight down into a black abyss. To the left a passageway turned upward. It was some ten feet high and two or three times as wide. It went up at an incline into the green, luminous darkness. They followed Degg. A mile perhaps, steadily climbing. Martt calculated. They had already walked possibly fifteen miles—and they were more than eight times the normal size of Zee's world. That was more than a hundred and twenty miles underground—most of it downward.

Martt realized that he was tired. And hungry. Before leaving Reaf he had thought of food necessary for this trip. Degg had a concentrated food—a dull brown powder. Martt promptly had appropriated it—had tested it to make sure it was not a size-drug....

The passages abruptly opened into black, empty space. A rocky slope rolling gently upward, strewn with huge black boulders. It extended as far as Martt could see, upward into a luminous darkness. Overhead was a black sky—murky with distance.

Degg stopped. "We begin getting large here."

Zee translated it to Martt.

"Let's eat, then," said Martt. "Zee, aren't you tired and hungry?"

There was water lying in flat pools on the rocks. It was clear, cold and sweet. They sat down, talking and eating. Then Zee slept. And Degg slept also.

Martt sat alert, watching, while the headless thing stretched itself somnolent on a rock near by, its single eye on the stalk wilting downward in drowsiness.

Martt strove to master his revulsion. He called softly, "Eeff! Eeff, come here!"

But it would not come. It moved farther away, whimpering to itself.

"Zee, wake up! We've got to get started. You've slept hours."

The real size-change now began. In single file they walked up the black slope. It shrank beneath them—creeping, crawling dwindling away under their feet. The boulders shrank into rocks, into pebbles. In an hour they were walking upon a smooth surface.

The black void was no longer empty. Mountains showed ahead—and to the sides. Giant faces of rock, looming into unfathomable distance of the black sky. The mountains were drawing closer; contracting, rushing down with a violent movement.

Martt apprehensively glanced behind. A wall of dwindling rock was coming after them. The drug in these larger doses seemed acting with a multiplied power. The scene was a dizzy swirl of movement. Mountains closing in everywhere. To Martt came a flash of terror. They would be crushed. Their bodies were growing tremendously to fill this constricted space.

Degg had stopped walking—they were gathered in a group. They were now in the center of a circular valley, with a ring of mountains closing in. A ten-mile valley... a mile... a hundred feet....

But the mountains shrank to hills; to a low cliff-wall—a ridge.... It closed in....

"Now!" shouted Degg. They leaped over the low ledge of encircling rock; scrambled over it and fell on a level ground above....

Beside them Martt saw a small jagged hole in the ground.... The size of his waist... his fist... his finger.... It dwindled, closed and was gone; while again, above them and all about, were black, empty spaces, filled soon with shrinking canyons out of which hastily they climbed....

A phantasmagoria of climbing, struggling upward to avoid being crushed by their own growth....

There was a canyon too narrow, with sides too high.... They had to stop their growth, and climb its jagged, precipitous side. The climb took hours There was another meal, while Martt slept and Zee remained on guard.

Then another valley. Broad, with a steeply inclined floor. They grew out of it; into another; and another....

Martt became conscious of a change in the air. Cooler, with a dankness. And now at last, overhead the void was no larger black. A suggestion of purple. And suddenly as they leaped from a chasm which shrank and closed under them, Martt saw a sky. Somber purple, with stars.

A new conception of it all swept Martt. His Earth—the stars of its Universe. The Inner Surface of the Atom, Zee's realm—millions of times larger. And now—compared to Reaf... was he now a million times the size of Reaf?... Or a million million? Largeness, unfathomable. A convex world out here.

The surface of a globe, whirling in Space. And overhead, still other stars, so gigantic—so remote!

Martt gazed curiously around, They were at last in Degg's world—the region of the Arcs. A tumbled land of crags upon which lay a gray-black snow. Martt's heart sank before its utter desolation—a tumbled waste, upheaved as though by some cataclysm of nature. Desolation! And as though to veil it, a fall of blackish snow—a somber, tragic shroud.

It was night. And, Martt surmised, a winter season. Yet the air was not cold; merely dank. And the snow seemed not cold, congealed perhaps by the dank, heavy air; but to Martt's touch, not cold, no more than chill.

With her bare limbs and filmy veiling, Zee was shivering. Martt discarded his jacket, but she did not want it.

He said, "But you must be cold, Zee."

"I'm not." She shook herself. "I'm—frightened. This—night up here—it's like a tomb, Martt."

Tomblike, indeed. A dank, chill silence brooded over the night. And then, almost unheralded, it was not night, but day. A small, cold-red sun leaped up from the distant black horizon. A day of dull, flat light. It stained the snow with blood....

Blood everywhere....

Degg said somberly to Zee, "Always blood. It is an omen... My land, doomed—" There was a quiver in Zee's voice as she repeated his words to Martt.

They had come now not to mistrust Degg. He seemed a well-meaning youth. Simple-minded. He had told them something of his world—of Rokk, and the woman Mobah. Degg, in his heart, hated and feared Rokk.

"Why?" demanded Zee.

He turned his dark, solemn eyes upon her. "You are too

gentle, little girl Zee, to understand. We have many—horrible things here in Arc. I would not talk of them with you."

It had been Rokk's plan, Degg said, to take Leela and Frannie to the place where he lived. Degg was to join Rokk there.... It was not so very far.... Degg called it Rokk's mound. They were headed that way now. Soon it would be night again—Martt could do what he thought was best toward rescuing the two girl prisoners. And Martt promised he would protect Degg.

Vaguely in Martt's mind had been the idea that he could use the drugs again now—make himself still larger—catch Rokk unawares. But the large drug would take no further effect. The maximum size had been reached. Degg did not know why; save that these drugs were for smallness—the large one merely an antidote to the other.

Martt was left without tangible plan. But his first desire was to get near Rokk's mound—whatever sort of place that might be. And he would decide then what could be done.

The blood-red sun came swiftly up in a low arc, and plunged as swiftly down again. To Martt, it had been some half an hour of daylight. Now came the brooding night—and in another half-hour the sun would again make its low sweep.

Martt urged Degg forward. Eeff was leading—lurid, green-white against the black of the ground. Then it stopped. Its eye quivered; it screamed—a long, shuddering, half-human cry of fright.

Degg stood frozen—a statue in the gloom. And then Martt—and Zee also, for she uttered a low, suppressed cry—saw what had frightened Eeff.

It was about a hundred feet away—a dull, glowing red as though the blood of sunlight were upon it. A thing which might have been a long, blood-red vine. Not animal, but vegetable. It lay on the ground—a great, thick stem, with up-flung leafy branches waving like tentacles. At intervals, upon long stalks, were round spots of green light. Gleaming, baleful eyes.

The thing was lying its length upon the ground. Not quiescent, but everywhere in quivering, undulating, snakelike movement. Its eyes seemed all turned this one way. Eyes suggesting an intelligence—a reasoning—behind them. A thing, not animal but vegetable! Its brain, lacking even the least vestige of human or animal restraint, cast in a mold unutterably horrible.

Eeff was crouching at Degg's feet, babbling with terror. Degg muttered, "It is unrooted! Free! It—I told Rokk they would break free some time—before he was ready!"

"Unrooted!" Zee echoed.

Unrooted! It was slithering, out there in the darkness... It shrank to a blood-red blur.... It vanished....

They went on again. Degg would not talk, save to reiterate fearsomely, "I knew they would cast off their roots! Roaming, everywhere. And Rokk thought he dared to grow them—"

A rise of ground lay ahead. Beyond its crest only the purple sky was visible, with stars sweeping in rapid, low arcs. Martt, Degg and Zee were walking together, with Eeff close before them.

Eeff began whimpering again; then screamed. And ahead, from over the crest of the hill, as though in answer came an echoing scream! Yet not an echo! A scream, human! It drove the blood to Martt's heart; stopped his breathing. The scream of a voice familiar—a girl's voice—Frannie!

For all the horror surging over him, Martt leaped forward. And stopped, stricken on the hill-crest.

Beneath him in the gloom lay a shallow, bowl-like depression. The starlight illumined it wanly. Frannie was down there, struggling in the grip of a blood-red, vegetable thing! A segment of it was wrapped around her, dragging her forward. The light of it drenched her with blood; its myriad green eyes glared throughout its waving length.

And ahead of it was a line of others of its kind, leading the way, slithering up and over the opposite slope.

6

THE BLOOD-RED DAY

To Frannie, the subterranean river was an inferno of roaring blackness. Her dhrane was whirled along, sometimes swimming, sometimes floundering desperately. Frannie clung to its antlers and closed her eyes... An eternity.... She heard Rokk shouting; felt the dhrane scrambling upon solid ground. The water dropped away from its sides....

Frannie found herself and her dhrane standing in a dull, luminous darkness upon a ledge by the river. The other dhranes were there. Rokk spoke to Leela.

"What does he say?" Fannie demanded.

"He says we must get larger—this is too dangerous."

They followed then the methods used afterward by Degg in guiding Martt and Zee. Wading, in a large size, they went down the river. Then into the passageway leading upward.

And then the climb into largeness. To Frannie it seemed unending; but though they were only an hour or two ahead of Martt in starting, they were several hours ahead when they reached the giant world. Frannie and Leela were near to exhaustion, even though they had ridden most of the way. Rokk had not paused to sleep.

It was day when they reached the desolate land of the Arcs. Then a tomblike night; then blood-red day again.

Rokk rode now with Frannie and Leela beside him, and the woman Mobah behind. Rokk was jubilant. He talked swiftly to Leela. At intervals, Leela translated.

"He says he is glad to have us. He is taking us to his house—his mound, he calls it. He says, very soon there is something important happening up here. He is going to take us—show us it—happening." Leela shuddered.

"What is going to happen?" Frannie demanded.

"I don't know. Something—sinister, horrible. You saw his face when he told me?"

Frannie had seen it, indeed, but she was striving to master her fear. There was something queerly sinister, inhuman, about Rokk. And his smile had a leer to it. Shining in his dark eyes, which often were fixed thoughtfully on Leela, there was a look Frannie could not fail to understand. The woman, Mobah, had noticed it. Once, over her broad expressionless face a torrent of passion had swept. Hate? Jealousy? It flashed at Leela—and at Frannie—and was instantly gone.

Frannie said now, "Ask him what he wants of us. Why did he ever go down into our world?"

Leela listened to Rokk's smiling explanation. The man's voice was soft, caressing. Leela went white.

"He says, Frannie—he says his world here is very harsh—not good to live in. There is very little food—he says that he and some other men—his followers—are planning to descend into my world and conquer it. Kill all its men—Frannie, don't you understand?—kill, just the men of my world—

"There was a silence. Then Leela added, with a frightened hush to her voice, "Up here all is bleak and terrible. The women are all like this woman behind us—unbeautiful—"

Rokk was riding faster now, and soon, as they ascended a rise of ground, his home came into view. It lay on a falling slope, with paths trodden in the snow about it—a bulging mound built of pressed blocks of the gray-black snow. It rose above the surface perhaps ten feet—an oblong mound twenty feet wide and five times as long, like the grave of some giant burial there, with a small upright chimney at its farther end for a headstone. A few rectangles of white marked its doors and windows as though one might care to stand on the ground and gaze down at the coffin entombed within. Near by, two other mounds lay like the graves of children, with beaten paths connecting them.

Rokk's home was set alone in the midst of this snowy waste! Frannie's heart was cold with apprehension. What was to be her fate—and Leela's—within?

At Rokk's call a half-grown boy appeared in a doorway of the main mound. He led the dhranes away, Frannie and Leela were taken down a crude flight of icy steps and into the mound. It was much longer than it appeared; it seemed to extend at least another story underground, for Frannie saw an incline leading downward.

They had entered the top story. Rokk led them along a passageway; Frannie saw low-roofed rooms, with ceilings curved to the mound. Each with a window opening at the ground level; and with crude furniture seemingly fashioned from stone blocks.

Into such a room Rokk ushered them. He was smiling, bowing like a friendly host; his words to Leela were suave. But in his eyes there was an unmistakable irony, and when Frannie hesitated at the door, he pushed her roughly.

Mobah had disappeared. Rokk stood a moment talking to Leela. The door to the passageway was open. Rokk and Leela had their backs to it. Frannie became aware that beyond the door Mobah was standing listening. And in the dimness there, Frannie caught a glimpse of the woman's intense face. It was torn with a jealous passion—a torrent of loosed passion debasing its calm stolidity into an aspect almost bestial.

The GIANT WORLD
by RAY CUMMINGS

He had no other thought than to kill.

As Rokk turned slightly, the lurking woman silently fled. Rokk bowed to Frannie, and to Leela—a bow ceremoniously grotesque, but with a dignity, nevertheless. His hand lingered on Leela's white arm, but Leela jerked away. He shrugged, smiled, and went through the door, barring it after him.

"Oh, Frannie!" Leela at last gave way. She sobbed with fright unrestrained: and this gave Frannie additional strength to be calm. She sat Leela on the couch—a railed slab of stone, with a litter of furs on it like the bed of an animal. She tried to comfort Leela. Then left her; tried the door softly. It was stoutly barred.

Then she tried the window. It had a pane as transparent as glass, but evidently unbreakable. Frannie struck it recklessly with her fist. And there seemed no way to open the window. Through it Frannie could see along the snow-covered ground outside. The night had just come. The ground was dark, with faint stars showing above.

Frannie sat on the bed with Leela. They were both so exhausted that for a time they slept. Hours, perhaps—Frannie never knew. Then she awoke. The scene in the room was unchanged. It was night again. Leela was awake. Frannie began questioning her as to what Rokk most recently had said. Leela was outwardly calm now.

"He—insists we are not to be harmed, Frannie. He told me— just before he left—that he wanted me to like him." A shiver ran over Leela's frail body. "He will work to make me like him— he will be very good to me. And you—he says there is a young man—that man he left back in Reaf—named Degg. He is sure Degg will like you, Frannie."

"Did he say any more about that important thing which is going to happen?"

"Yes. He said he is going to take us somewhere—as soon as we have rested, and Degg has come to join us here. Take us somewhere—where we shall see a wonderful awesome sight. Frannie, he told me the men here in this world do not like their women. He has brought me and you—to show us to the men—that they may see how beautiful women can be. Then— they will join him to go down into smallness—to conquer—"

Leela choked. She added, and a hush fell upon her voice: "Frannie, this Rokk has planned it all. He says there is too little food here. The women—and the children that the men no longer want to feed—are all placed apart. Exiled to a city— where he is going to take us. And show us—"

A tapping at the window checked her. The girls stared at each other with the blood draining from their faces. A gentle tapping from outside. A scraping, fumbling as though soft fingers were working at the window.

Frannie stood up, trembling. Then she moved along the wall, and with her face to the window, peered out. The tapping had stopped. Outside she saw a faint, lurid red glow. And three gleaming spots of green. Moving, peering. And then like the tendrils of a creeping vine, a leafy something, with a red sheen upon it, gently beating at the pane; tapping—fumbling.

Frannie drew back. "Leela—out there—" But another sound stopped her. Someone—something—was unbarring the door of their room! The two girls were frozen with terror, incapable of sound or movement. A bar dropping with a muffled thump! The door slowly began opening inward....

It was the woman Mobah. Her face was grim; her dull eyes were smoldering green-black coals. She flung a menacing glance at the girls, moved swiftly across the room. Her fingers at the pane touched some hidden lock. The window swung open.

Mobah darted back, seized Leela, tried to shove her toward Frannie and the window. Leela screamed, resisted, fought with all her little strength and called a warning to Frannie.

But it was too late. Through the window a thick, red-glowing tentacle came slithering. Its green eyes were waving triumphantly. It caught Frannie; rolled back upon itself, jerking her upward.

Heavy steps sounded in the passageway outside the room, and Rokk's alarmed voice, shouting. Rokk burst in. He knocked Mobah aside with a blow of his fist, and swept Leela protectingly backward.

The segment of red thing within the room slithered out the window, carrying Frannie with it.

"**She is** gone, my lady Leela, It is unfortunate, but we can not help" it. She is lost—we shall never see her again."

Leela and Rokk, were alone in the room. Leela shrank upon the couch; against his gaze she huddled with a corner of the robe drawn to shield her white limbs. He stood before her.

"Gone, Leela. Dead, by now… Don't shudder, little white woman. It is the law of life—some live, some die…. But Degg will be sorry."

She had no word, no heart with which to answer.

He went on, with a frown crossing his face. "That vegetable thing coming here has changed my plans. It has no right to be unrooted. I grew it, Lady Leela—and many others of its kind—for a certain purpose. But now it has broken away, before I was quite ready to dig it up. It thinks it is full-grown. It is conscious of its power. And that which during all its growth I have taught it, to do—" He shrugged. "I suppose they have all broken loose. All roaming—" A horrible grimness came to Rokk's voice. "Well, they will do what I taught them—we shall have to hurry if we wish to see it, Lady Leela."

Leela summoned words. "To see—what?"

He smiled. "You are impatient—and as becomes only a woman—curious! You shall see, little white woman—blood-red things—" He gestured. "Enough of that. But you shall realize how great is Rokk. I planned it all. But now I shall have to change my plans a little. I had wanted to show you and your friend—the little Frannie—to the men of this world. So that they—our men—would know how beautiful women can be. There is no time now, with the red things broken loose. We shall have to be careful, my Leela. I shall send word to all the men everywhere to have a care… I wish Degg would come—but we can not wait for him now…. There are animals, too, who should be guarded from these roaming red vines I have grown. You have not seen our animals, Leela? Degg has one—a very friendly thing; we call it Eeff. It is but half human—and only half materialized into substance. A loyal friend, if it likes you. But its mentality is that of an imbecile…. I talk too much, like a loose-tongued woman. There is no time—we must start."

He called roughly, "Mobah! Come here at once!"

The woman appeared, sullen, defiant. On the flesh of her heavy gray shoulder was a red bruise where Rokk had struck her.

"Mobah! Bring the dhranes. We are leaving for the Ice City. Tell my boy here to have Degg follow us when he comes… hurry!…"

They rode fast. Alternate night and day—endless frozen wastes. Occasionally they passed single mounds, isolated like that of Rokk. Others in groups; blood-stained graveyards by day—eerie and gruesome in the starlight. Leela saw many of the green-white animals, lurking like werewolves prowling among the mounds. And there were men gazing curiously at the travelers. To them often Rokk gave a warning that the vegetable things were loose.

But he said to Leela, "There really is no danger. These things I have grown will do my purpose in the Ice City. Then I will command them back to their fields. Let them rot there harmlessly in a red welter. I can control them. They know me for their creator—their master."

There were few women or girls to be seen about the mounds. Rokk said, with a horrible irony, "We have sent most of them to the Ice City. It is a very beautiful place—we men have sent our women there. The women—" He laughed sarcastically. "They are very stupid. They do not guess our purpose."

They rode in silence. Then Rokk spoke again. "My woman,

Mobah"—he glanced behind at the patient figure riding behind them—"I have kept Mobah with me. She is good to work in the mound. But you, my Lady Leela—" He chucked. "We shall get rid of Mobah all in good Time. We do not want her around, do we? But I will not make you work, Leela, In your city of Crescent, little white woman, you and I will be very great people. I shall be the leader of all our men—"

Again Leela did not answer.

A red day plunged into night. Far to the left across the snowy wastes to the distant horizon, Leela saw a white radiance in the sky. A vague patch of silver, as of light reflected from some remote distance below the horizon. Rokk waved his hand.

"You see that, Leela? That is where I found the drugs. This globe is very fair, off there. Longer days and nights. A warm, fruitful summer. Food is there. Trees, with fruit. But it is all owned by another race of people. They will not let us in. They are very powerful—very far advanced in civilization. A wonderful age of science.... They know everything. I crept into one of their cities and stole the drugs."

To Leela then was driven home the conception of how vast is God's great plan of the Universe. This miserable region owned by Rokk's people was no more than the Polar waste of this globe. A fairer land of science lay there where the distant radiance showed. A great, cultured civilization perhaps. And farther beyond it—other races—all on this one tiny globe whirling among these stars....

They came at last within sight of the City of Ice. In the starlight it glittered with a pale sheen. It stood on a broad plateau above the surrounding valleys—a place of white spires, glittering under the stars, the whole surrounded by a high white wall of ice.

And as they came closer, Leela saw within the city a yellow-red glare. Behind it, a high tower of stone dominated the scene; the glare painted the tower a yellow-red upon one side. "The pit of fire," said Rokk. "The one place in all our realm where the fires underground come near the surface. It brings a warmth—a beauty. You shall see." Ha laughed his horrible laugh. "That is why we tell the women they should like it here—"

They approached the wall. Rokk gazed around. "We are but just in time." In the farther distance beyond the city was a red sheen against the ground. Rokk understood it, though at the moment Leela did not. "Just in time, little woman. I had thought we might better enter by the tunnel under the wall. But that is not necessary."

They rode through a gate, plunged at once into a passageway, and emerged presently within the stone tower, left the dhranes there, and mounted the tower. At its top, Rokk stood with Leela. Mobah sullenly was behind them. Rokk glanced back at her. He said softly, "I think perhaps she guesses what is to happen. But she can do nothing about it."

Presently Mobah moved away and disappeared. Rokk patted his belt. "I have all the drugs here, Leela. All there are in this whole realm—except a very little of each which I left with Degg. We must guard them carefully."

To Leela came the thought that she might gain possession of the drugs and thus escape. But Rokk was very watchful

They stood upon a broad balcony, with the single tower room behind them and a breast-high parapet in front. At the parapet, Leela gazed down. From this height the city lay spread beneath them. It was still night. A simple, placid scene, quiet, and in a measure beautiful. A few broad streets of packed, gray-black snow. Flat, oblong houses of ice blocks which were white and glittering, with spires and minarets occasionally adorning them.

Directly beneath Leela, at the foot of the tower, was a yawning yellow-red pit. She could see directly down into it; a glare, some great distance down to where the fires of the earth were broken out. Rising wisps of smoke... a sulfurous, fiery breath... and a torrent of grateful heat surging upward.

Around the pit, the city was built of stone for a distance, like a broad, square park. Trees were growing there; huge, graceful ferns; blue-green leaves like great flopping ears of an animal. And giant palms, hung with purple fruit.... A tropical garden, with flower-lined, winding paths.... By contrast with all this bleak region Leela had seen, the single little park was very beautiful.

There were a few women moving about the city—dull, heavy-looking, shapeless women robed in a monotone of drab garments. Uninspired of aspect, Yet each had a soul... desires... longings....

In the park a woman sat and played with a little girl. There was another woman, newly arrived here, with a baby at her breast....

Rokk's voice broke upon Leela's thoughts with a rasp. "But who is to feed them? It gets very tiresome, giving them food.... Ah! Now you shall see my solution, Lady Leela—"

Beyond the city walls, out over the starlit, snowy wastes, spots of red sheen were visible. Moving. Coming nearer. Spots of red sheen resolving into long, thin lines of red. Undulating, twisting, slithering forward. Green spots of eyes, waving, peering.

Red, growing things unrooted. Coming monstrously to do that for which during all their growth they had been trained. There seemed thousands of them. Over every distant slope they came closing in upon the city. Thick red vines a hundred feet long. Others grown into a tangled clump, every separate tendril of which was in slimy movement. A red boll, like the bulging trunk of a tree. It rolled, leaped. Another of a flat, round central growth, with prickling spines like huge needles standing erect, and waving, groping tentacles. It hitched itself along, awkwardly.

They came from everywhere. Red, gleaming monsters of the ground, advancing with a grim, uncanny silence, closing in upon the city.

Leela watched, with the blood freezing in her veins, within the city no alarm had sounded. The woman in the park played with her little girl. But the baby at the other woman's breast was crying....

The first of the red things reached the city wall. Slithered up like some monstrous red ivy growing there. A thing of dangling green pods from which a slimy juice was dripping. A segment of it raised high over the wall, with green eyes staring down.

In a nearby street a headless, friendly animal gave out its imbecilic cry. The two women in the park looked and saw, and screamed....

The red thing rose and slithered over the wall. Stretched its length down a street; then encircled a house, its wide-flung segments slithering into every door and window. Screams from in there sounded over the silent, starlit city. Shrill, throat-tearing screams of women... and the piping, terrified cries of children....

The alarm spread. The cries were caught up, echoed from everywhere about the city. Women and girl children were rushing in a panic from the houses....

Over the wall at its every point, the red things were climbing... spreading over the city... filling the streets... climbing with a red, leafy growth into houses... green peering eyes, searching everywhere....

One of the flat, round growths with prickling spines—needles each as long as a human body—lurched itself into the park. With a sudden spring it caught a running woman. Its tentacles tossed her aloft. She fell, impaled upon its sword-like spines. Its tentacles pulled an arm from her body... tossed the arm away.... The woman was still screaming—horribly....

Leela, sickened, covered her face with her hands. She heard Rokk's gloating voice, "You see—my solution? Look, little white woman! Make your heart stout, like Rokk's. This is the law of life. Some live, some die. We—you and I—will live, for love, when this blood-red day is over."

Day! The dawn had come. The red sun rose from the horizon in its low arc. Red, staining everything.

Leela, with a fascination, again involuntarily stared. The city was a chaos of terror. From windows, with reason fled, women were leaping. The red things caught them as they fell....On a flat housetop a woman crouched with a baby in her arms, and a little girl huddling at her knees. A slim red arm came up over the parapet of roof. Other red things came up, and poised with watching green eyes. The woman fought the red arm with all her meager strength. It seized the baby, waved the small, gray-white body aloft, dashed it to a red pulp against the stone of the parapet. Other arms jerked the little girl away. A flat, red thing engulfed the woman and sat mouthing and tearing....

In the park a crowd of the women were huddled. Some were trying to climb the high railing at the pit of fire, but could not. The red things slithered among them....

The blood-red day! A white, glittering city, stained crimson now. Splashed and stained; and upon it the red sun poured a polluting, gory light....

The blood-red day....

7

THE FIGHT ON THE PARAPET

Martt stood in the starlight at the top of the slope, frozen into immobility with horror. Fannie was struggling in the grip of the red vine, being dragged along, with others of its kind leading the way. Grown and taught for nothing but the blood-red day of the Ice City, these things with single purpose were dragging Fannie there. Martt stood stricken for an instant. The red thing paused. All its green eyes turned. Beyond it the other things came to a stop, irresolute, and then slithered on. But the one with Frannie lay momentarily quiescent; only its eyes were quivering.

Martt became aware that Zee and Degg were beside him. Eeff was crouching at its master's feet, whimpering with terror. Martt shouted, "Zee, run back! Come on. Degg!"

He caught a glimpse of Degg's face, gray with fright. But his eyes showed a sudden determination. And Degg leaped, with Martt after him.

The red thing flung up its forward tentacles, and shoved Frannie farther back within its folds. Degg leaped for the clump of its branches where Frannie was entangled.

Martt, running forward, abruptly stopped. One of the drug cylinders within his pockets had bumped his thigh. A thought swept him—the drug for smallness! He stopped, recklessly poured from the cylinder nearly half its contents. And stood, with a huge buckle of his jacket, crushing the white tablets into a powder in his hand.

Degg had fought his way to Frannie. He had torn her loose, thrust her violently away, but was himself entrapped. He fought, ripping, tearing at the red branches, struggling to avoid the sinuous tentacles which curled back at him. A thick tendril of the vine had wound itself about his legs....

With the powder in his left hand, Martt rushed forward. There was a part of the red thing which seemed of lesser size and strength. Martt rushed in among its lashing brambles. They entwined him. He ducked the sweep of a tentacle thick as his body. Eyes on the branches peered into his face. He seized one, pulled it off. A slime with a red phosphorescence was on his fingers. A pod struck his face; he tore it open and scattered its seeds. A red, noisome juice spattered him.

Martt was fighting only with his right hand. One of his legs was gripped and held; he kicked, striving to free it.

These smaller branches were easily broken. They mashed, some of them like a porous tropical plant, oozing sap. They were spongy. Martt scattered a little of the white powder; sifted it through his fingers. The vegetable growth sucked it up—the drug mingled with the sap of its bruises.

The branches were dwindling. Upon vegetable matter the drug acted mores swiftly than upon animal cells. The smaller tendrils shriveled. Then branches of greater thickness. Martt could feel them letting go their hold—shrinking, loosening their grip.

Around him in a moment was a shriveled, shrunken bramble. He kicked himself free. A huge tentacle from another portion licked back and seized him; whirled him aloft. But he kept his wits. Tore at it with his fingers; rubbed the drug into its bruised bark. Along all its length, the drug acted. Martt's weight brought its shriveled strength to the ground. He fell upon his feet; tore himself loose again. Stamped and tore, and leaped away.

Throughout all the length of the monstrous vine, now, the drug was acting. Martt momentarily stood inactive, panting. He saw that Degg had freed Frannie—saw her and Zee huddled at a distance on the slope nearby. Degg was still fighting; one of his legs seemed queerly twisted; an arm of the red vine held him, but he kept his feet. Eeff was darting forward and back, too much terrified to approach, yet anxious to help.

The vine everywhere was shrinking. Martt ran to free Degg. But he was too late. The largest remaining tentacle lashed forward; it caught Degg, whirled him up in the air and flung him heavily to the ground. Degg lay still.

A moment. Then the vine was so shriveled that Martt waded throughout its lashing length. Tore it apart. Scattered it. Stamped upon its twisting, slithering red segments.

All dwindling. Separate, dismembered segments quivering around him... smaller... red, twisting lines, with tiny green eyes... They winked and vanished into smallness....

"Is he dead? Oh, Martt, do you think he is dead?"

They bent over Degg and he opened his eyes. Martt knelt and lifted his head. It was evident that he was dying; and evident, too, that he knew it. He spoke, laboriously whispered words in Zee's language. He tried to gesture toward Zee; on his face was an earnestness, almost a desperation lest he might fail to give his dying message.

Martt said, "Zee, he's trying to talk to you. Bend closer—he's talking."

Zee knelt at his head. He was panting, struggling breathlessly with each word. "Rokk—was going to take your sister Leela to the—City of Ice. Now that the red things are loose—I think you will find—him and her—there."

His breath ended with a long sigh. But he began again. "Eeff will lead you. Tell Eeff—to take you through the—tunnel into the—stone tower. And—hurry!"

His eyes closed. Then they opened very wide. They tried to focus on Zee's face. She bent lower to hear his faint whisper. "Hurry! You understand—about Leela, there with Rokk. He means, for her, a thing very terrible. You must—hurry." He added, with a breath so faint she barely heard his words, "You are—so very beautiful, little Zee. I never saw—any woman so beautiful. But I am not Rokk—I could not have harmed you."

He stiffened just a trifle; then went limp, his head with staring eyes dangling backward over Martt's arm.

Martt laid him gently on the ground. Eeff went and sat by him, crying softly.

It was red day when they approached the City of Ice. Eeff had led them, as Degg suggested. They saw the city from far off, with a red glow staining its white glitter. Then Eeff plunged them into a black tunnel. It seemed miles. Then it ascended, and they emerged into a wave of heat, with a yellow-red glare beside them.

They were at the bottom of a tall stone tower; a doorway was near at hand, Martt gazed up the tower's side. A man was up there, behind a parapet, gazing out at the city: a man's head and shoulders, queerly foreshortened. But Martt recognized him.

Rokk!

Martt pushed Zee and Frannie hastily into the tower. He commanded, "You two stay here, with Eeff. I'm going up. You stay here."

Again Martt thought of the drug cylinders he was carrying. He drew them from his pockets, handed them swiftly to Zee. "Keep these. Whatever happens—if I don't come back—use them. Eeff will lead you home. To Reaf. Ask it if it can lead you."

Zee said, in her own language, "Eeff, come here. Can you lead me back—down there where we meet Degg in that place called Reaf? You remember? Where the water was?"

The headless thing turned its eye upon her. It chattered, "Yes, I remember. I can go there—but I want Degg. I want to go back to Degg."

Martt, alone, mounted the circular incline softly, and as swiftly as he dared. Had Rokk seen him? He did not think so. Was Leela up there?... If he could get behind Rokk unobserved....

Half-way up there was an oval window in the tower through which Martt caught his first view of the interior of the city.

The sun was sinking at the horizon. The end of the blood-red day! A silence had fallen with the falling sun. A crimson city, strewed with what had once been living, human flesh and blood—dismembered now... strewn... unnameable....

And climbing the walls; red monsters slithering away—seeking other horrors.

The silent nightfall of the blood-red day.

Martt's gorge rose. He turned from the window, and mounted the incline.

The room at the top was circular, with many windows. An empty room of stone, almost dark, with the starlight streaming in dimly to illumine it.

Martt crept softly. Through a doorway he could see Rokk's figure on the balcony outside. And another figure. Leela, white of face, with her black hair streaming, and her tattered, dirt-stained veiling falling about her. Leela! She was standing, half turned, shuddering with horror. She saw Martt! Surprise; wonderment, joy mirrored her face. His fingers went to his lips warningly. But not quite in time. She uttered a low cry, instantly checked.

Rokk swung about. He, too, saw Martt; he stiffened, with his shoulders flung back against the parapet and his jaw dropping. Martt had instantly leaped, but Rokk met him squarely, surged forward, and they fell.

Rokk was the stronger; Martt knew it at once. He rolled, desperately struggling to come on top, with his legs braced against the floor. But Rokk flung him off and regained his feet.

Instantly Martt was up, quicker, lighter than his antagonist. He struck for Rokk's face, missed and then caught Rokk full on the chest with his fist. The man staggered, but he was not hurt. Rokk's swing went wide, as Martt nimbly ducked. Again they came together. Surged across the balcony, kicking, tearing, seeking each other's throats. Locked, with legs entwined they struck the parapet, rebounded, fell and rolled together to the opposite wall. A primitive struggle of men using only the weapons with which nature had endowed them. Fighting grimly, almost silently, each with no thought but to kill.

Leela, near by, stood helpless, confused, a hand pressed against her mouth in terror. There was a sound, a startled outcry. Frannie and Zee were in the tower room, with Eeff cowering behind them.

Martt momentarily was on top of his adversary, with Rokk's hairy hand beneath his chin, pressing his head back. Martt ripped the hand away. He called, "Run! Run—all of you!"

Rokk heaved him backward, half rose, and surged over on top. Martt saw vaguely another figure appear on the balcony. A heavy, gray-faced woman. He heard Rokk pant, "Mobah!"

The Woman leaped upon the scene. She avoided Zee and Frannie. She strove to get at Martt. She kicked; she tried to strike at him. He heard Zee's voice, "Frannie! Leela! Help me!" As he fought, he was aware that the three girls were pulling at the woman—pulling her away, holding her.

Martt momentarily had slackened his efforts. Rokk's fist caught him in the face, dazed him. Martt felt Rokk lifting him up, heaving him. His body struck the three-foot-wide, level top of the parapet. He clung desperately, as Rokk leaped up to throw him off.

They were locked together, rolling on the parapet top! Martt at its edge, his head momentarily over, felt a wave of heat—saw, far down, the red-yellow glare. Rokk suddenly tried to cast him loose. Then was pushing. They were both lying at the edge.

Scrambling. Panting. And suddenly Zee was up on the parapet, crouching—her frail white hands gouging at Rokk's face. It confused him. He relaxed. Martt gave one last desperate surge. He saw, and felt Rokk's body slipping, sliding over the edge, feet first. Rokk's hold on Martt was torn away, by his own weight, and by Zee's frenzied plucking fingers. His face, close to Martt's for an instant, showed wide, terrified eyes; a mouth that gaped.

His hold broke. His body slid. He was gone! Martt lay panting at the edge, with Zee's steadying grip upon him. A cry sounded. A wail. The woman Mobah had torn loose from Frannie and Leela. She leaped to the parapet. Poised for an instant—a grim, gray statue of despair. Bereft of reason, she called, "Rokk! Rokk!" And with a long, shuddering cry, she plunged.

There was silence for a moment on the parapet. No one looked down. And from over the distant, desolate horizon, presently the red sun came up with the dawn of a new day.

8

YOUTH!

Life is very strange. Brett, and I—Frank Elgon of the Interplanetary Mail—of full maturity, at the peak of our physical and mental strength—how inglorious were the parts we played! So inconsequential I scarcely have the heart to recount our futile actions. Yet we thought always that we were doing our best.

We stood there beside the arcade, helplessly watching Frannie and Leela disappear into smallness. Brett left me to guard the spot. He rushed away; came back to tell me that the giant wading in the lake was gone, that he could not find Martt or Zee.

For a time we watched the small pebble beneath which Leela and Frannie had vanished. We even dared to move it carefully, but we could not see them.

The island was emptying of its people. We thought that Martt and Zee might have gone home. We decided to go and join them. Perhaps to take our vehicle, make it small to search for Leela, since we had no drugs.

I told Brett of his father's death. And it was well advanced into the morning before we learned that people on the island had seen Martt and Zee sailing for Reaf. Hours during which we had aimlessly searched, and prepared the vehicle for its trip into smallness to try and find Leela and Frannie.

Martt and Zee had sailed for Reaf! Following the giant! We had thought of doing that, to try and obtain the drugs. But it had seemed reckless, foolhardy, impossible of success. Yet

Martt had done it without hesitation. There is a caution comes at thirty which does not hamper twenty-one.

We procured a boat... Provisioned it. And sailed for Reaf, armed with our flash-cylinders. And there we found a huge belt lying on the rocks near a scattered wreck of buildings strewn upon the water.

Martt's belt, of a size which showed us he had used the drug! He had left the belt to explain that he had gone on to the giant world.

But we were utterly helpless! We could not follow him. We were starting aimlessly toward the river, when along the rocks there, we saw four moving figures. Normal in size. Martt, returning with the three girls! All of them tattered, bruised, bloodstained, their garments dirty and torn. But unharmed.

They waved at us. We landed and ran along the rocks. Martt's smile was tired, but very happy.

"Here they are, Brett. I brought them back—Zee and I did— here they are." He added, "We had a headless thing named Eeff. It led us back, but just now at the last, it ran away. It said it wanted to find Degg. It ran, forgetting it needed the drugs. A half-witted, cowardly sort of thing, but I liked it. Oh, there is so much to tell you—"

Deeds of youth! No caution, no pondering! Glorious deeds of youth, unfettered by maturity! No theory—just accomplishment!

Frannie was saying to me, "Oh Frank—" I held out my hand, but she flung herself upon me. "Frank, I—I've wanted so to get back to you!"

She clung to me. Her arms went around my neck. She was kissing me! Me, Frank Elgon! Poor as a guider of the lower traffic and just now proved so inglorious of action. But Frannie was kissing me! And whispering, "Oh, Frank, I love you!

Don't you know it? Haven't you always known it? You'd never say it to me. Please—please say it now!"

I murmured, "I love you, Frannie!" And held her close. That this could happen to me, ineffectual Frank Elgon!

Our last evening in Crescent. We were all going to the Earth— all but old Greedo. Brett and Leela had decided to be married on Earth. Fannie and I also, for Frannie did not seem to care how poor I was. Greedo wanted to go; but he said he was too old. A visit to Earth for his daughters, and then he hoped we would come back. Our last evening. I chanced to go alone to the roof-top of Greedo's home. Its banks of flowers were vivid in the twilight. A breeze rustled the tall potted ferns. The stars overhead were glowing with a silver radiance, mirrored in the distant, placid waters of the lake. Within the house downstairs, Leela's softly singing voice floated up.

Two figures sat in the starlight, among the flowers. Zee and Martt; close together, with his arm around her, and her head against his side, the tangle of her dark hair enveloping him.

I heard him say, awkwardly but very tenderly, "Three couples can be married at once, on Earth, Zee. Let's do that. Shall we?"

And heard her answering whisper, "Yes. Let's."

I tiptoed silently away.

ABOUT THE AUTHOR

"**He is** a Verne returned and Wells going forward," remarked "Bob" Davis, dean of American magazine editors. "He is the American H.G. Wells," say other critics.

Cummings has an unusual flair for things scientific as evidenced by the fact that while at Princeton University

Ray Cummings

he accomplished the remarkable feat of absorbing three years of physics in that many months. His five years' association with Thomas A. Edison as the latter's personal assistant also added to Cummings's scientific knowledge. His bizarre early life, living on orange plantations in Puerto Rico, striking oil in Wyoming, gold seeking in British Columbia, timber cruising in the North, before he was twenty, also left its imprint.

Leaving Mr. Edison's employ, Cummings began writing scientific fiction for many magazines. His stories gripped the popular imagination and they "clicked." Mr. Cummings's success as a writer has been meteoric, for in a few years he has become one of the world's most popular authors of scientific fiction.

Yet when asked about his own life and experiences Mr.

Cummings is shy and evasive. He would much rather talk about Miss Betty Starr Cummings, his four-year-old daughter, whom he terms "the really interesting member of the family."

A few of her exploits include being wrecked and trans-shipped in a heavy sea; adrift with her parents in a disabled open boat when only three weeks old; traveling thousands of miles by automobile, train and steamer; weathering a Florida hurricane and coming safely through an automobile accident. From all of which we can see that Mr. Cummings leads rather an adventurous life himself!

Winter finds him at home in Bermuda, but when the temperature starts to rise he quickly makes tracks for Quebec. As we write this a letter arrives from Bermuda announcing that his next full length fantastic novel will soon be ready for *Argosy* readers.

In the office of *Fantastic Novels* the other day, Mr. Cummings looked this autobiography over with a smile. "It's all right," he said, "except that Betty is fourteen and has already sold a story of her own, which she wrote when she was thirteen. Fulton Oursler accepted it for *Liberty Magazine!*"

Asked about how he came to write "The Girl in the Golden Atom," Mr. Cummings said that it was the very first thing that he ever wrote, and that he did it simply because he felt like putting down and developing the idea of entering a world inside a ring. He had no thought of selling it, nor even that it might be a usable story. Two friends, William C. McNulty, an important American etcher, and Spring Byington, motion picture actress (known nowadays as *the mother* in "The Jones Family" on the radio) looked over the story, and liked it. Mr. Cummings, who knew no rules for writing but simply put it down "straight from the heart" read it aloud to Mr. McNulty and to Miss Byington when either of them asked how it was coming along. They were very enthusiastic and urged him to take it to a publisher. Bob Davis snapped it up.

And Ray Cummings has been writing ever since.

www.ingramcontent.com/pod-product-compliance
Lightning Source LLC
Chambersburg PA
CBHW030546030726
47495CB00004B/1157